Anne Lady Halkett

The Autobiography of Anne Lady Halkett

Anne Lady Halkett

The Autobiography of Anne Lady Halkett

ISBN/EAN: 9783337113247

Printed in Europe, USA, Canada, Australia, Japan

Cover: Foto ©Raphael Reischuk / pixelio.de

More available books at **www.hansebooks.com**

THE AUTOBIOGRAPHY

OF

ANNE LADY HALKETT.

EDITED BY

JOHN GOUGH NICHOLS, F.S.A., &c.

PRINTED FOR THE CAMDEN SOCIETY.

M.DCCC.LXXV.

WESTMINSTER :
PRINTED BY NICHOLS AND SONS,
25, PARLIAMENT STREET.

[NEW SERIES XIII.]

INTRODUCTION.

NOTE BY THE DIRECTOR.—Where there are obvious mistakes in the text I have made the correction which Mr. Nichols would have made in revising his MS. noting at the foot his original words. I have also added a few words at the end, founded on the Life published at Edinburgh. Mr. Nichols has left a large number of notes, of which he would doubtless have made ample use, and he had collected a number of Lady Halkett's Meditations, of which a few specimens are printed in the Appendix.

This fragment of Lady Halkett's autobiography having been printed without comment, it appears to the Editor the most convenient course to take a review of its contents, and to combine with a summary thereof such other particulars derived from collateral sources as may at once enlighten the obscurity in which Lady Halkett studiously wrote, and also enable the reader to appreciate more thoroughly the value of the historical information which she actually imparts.

Lady Halkett is already known in the catalogue of female authors from the publication of some of her religious writings which was made in the year 1701, and from the " Life " which is prefixed to them. That life was derived in part from the a[uto-biography] now printed. [It was re-published in 1778][a] and it appears in an abridged shape in Ballard's Memoirs of Learned Ladies, 4to. 17[52], and 8vo. 17[75].

Anne Murray was born in London on the 4th of January, 1622, the younger daughter of Thomas Murray,[b] the preceptor and sub-

---

[a] In MS. "and pn in 1778." Amongst Mr. Nichols's notes there is the copy of the title-page of the " Meditations on the twenty-fifth Psalm." But I have not seen it, and as it is not mentioned here I conclude that it does not contain the title.—S. R. G.

[b] From some unaccountable misapprehension the biographer of 1701 calls him " Mr. Robert Murray " instead of Thomas; an error which is followed by Ballard and his copyists.

sequently Secretary to Prince Charles (afterwards King Charles I.), by Jane Drummond. In the memoirs now printed she commences her narrative by allusion to her parents, of whose extraction she declares she had no reason to be ashamed, as her father was descended from the family of the Earl of Tillebardine, and her mother from that of the Earl of Perth. The former dignity was conferred only in 1606, and the latter in 1605, therefore it was only collaterally that her parents could be related to those earls, nor has the degree of Lady Halkett's consanguinity to them been ascertained.

Her father, Thomas Murray, was already tutor to Charles Duke of York in 1605, when that prince was [in his fifth year].[a] An annuity of two hundred marks was granted to him on the 28th June in that year,[b] the patent for which he surrendered on the 27th Jan. 1613-14.

Little more than a twelvemonth after, Anne Murray lost her mother. There was probably some notice of this event in the leaf now lost from the manuscript,[c] which will be partially supplied by the following passage from the printed Life of 1701:

—— Her mother's affections who ——— ever after treated her more as a friend than a child, and sometime before her death made over to her, by assignation, a bond of the Earl of Kinnoul of 2,000 *lib. ster.*, which she received with all gratitude, as a new obligation to be more dutiful and diligent in attending upon her, especially being now more infirm and sickly; which, with great care and concern, she performed, ministering to her all the spiritual and bodily help she was capable to afford. This made a very comfortable and indearing impression upon her dying mother, and filled her heart with joy in finding not only the tender affection of her daughter, but much more, the

[a] Five (?) years of age.—MS.
[b] Rymer's Fœdera, xvi. 631.　　　　[c] See p. 19.

refreshing fruits of her piety and devotion. She died the 28 August, 1647, and was buried near her husband in the Savoy church.

On the 4th January, 160[9?], Mr. Murray received an additional reward in the sinecure office of Master of Sherburn Hospital, near Durham, to which "he was collated by dispensation, contrary to the statute;"[a] but he retained the position until his death.

In August, 1621, he was involved in temporary disgrace in consequence of his having allowed his royal pupil to receive and peruse, without the King's knowledge, a treatise which had been written by Dr. George Hakewill,[b] one of the Prince's chaplains, in opposition to the suggested match of his Highness with the Infanta of Spain. The doctor, William Hakewill his brother, Mr. Murray, and others who were privy to this business, were sent to the Tower of London.

By this well-intentioned but injudicious effort Dr. Hakewill's promotion was effectually checked, for he never attained higher preferment than that of the Archdeaconry of Surrey, which he held previously, and he was dismissed the Prince's service; but Mr. Murray probably substantiated his non-complicity to the King's satisfaction, for, within a very few months, he received the important favour of being nominated to the Provostship of Eton upon the death of the learned Sir Henry Saville. His election to that office was made on the 23rd February, 1621-2.

In 1622, only a twelvemonth after his temporary disgrace, we find him feasting the Marquis of Buckingham at Eton College, the Spanish match being then publicly acknowledged and regarded as likely[c] to be accomplished. But Mr. Murray's enjoyment of his good fortune was short. He died on the 9th April, 1623, at the

---

[a] Surtees's History of Durham, i. 142. [The date is not given here, but it is stated that his predecessor died in Dec. 1608].

[b] See the Life of Hakewill in Wood, Athenæ Oxon. (edit. Bliss) iii. 254.

[c] Letter of Mr. Chamberlain to Sir Dudley Carleton [Aug. 10, 1622] in Court and Times of James I. ii. 325.

age of fifty-nine, having yielded to the effects of an operation for the stone.[a]

[More than a year previously, on February 23, 1621-2, Bishop Williams being required as Lord Keeper to seal the patent for Murray's presentation, wrote to the Marquis of Buckingham a letter conveying a remonstrance that the provostship should have been conferred upon a layman, as it carried with it the cure of souls of the parish of Eton.]

The authoress gives an interesting account of her education (p. 2); and, describing her occasional recreation in the Spring Garden by St. James's Park (her mother had a house in St. Martin's Lane), waives all other particulars (p. 19) of her childish actions[b] until the time when her affections were first engaged, at the age of twenty-one, in 1644.

The young gentleman was a brother of her most intimate female friend, with whom she was frequently associated at the house of her sister Lady Newton, at Charlton, near Woolwich. He was Thomas Howard, the eldest son and heir apparent of Edward Lord Howard of Escrick, but any idea of a marriage with him was entirely discountenanced by her mother, because the Lord Howard's fortune was such as had need of a more considerable portion for his son than her mother could give her, or else it would ruin his younger children (p. 7). The history of this courtship occupies several pages, including a remarkable incident of Mr. Howard being treacherously and cruelly assaulted at Charlton by one Musgrove, the occupier of that estate during its sequestration, who mistook

---

[a] In MS. "Archbishop Williams took the occasion to write to the Duke(?) of Buckingham conveying a remonstrance that the Provostship should have been conferred upon a layman."— Williams's Letter is in Cabala, 264.

[b] The biographer of 1701, from some other manuscript of Lady Halkett, supplies several anecdotes of her childhood; but they are of trifling importance and no historical interest.

him for Sir Henry Newton, its Cavalier owner. At length Mr. Howard is sent away to France, but not until the lovers had mutually pledged their constancy (p. 13).

His absence did not lessen her mother's anger, and " for fourteen months she never gave me her blessing" (p. 14). Wearied with her bitterness, Anne Murray appealed to Sir Patrick Drummond, a cousin of her mother's, in order to procure admission to a Protestant nunnery in Holland (p. 15). Sir Patrick, "who was a wise and discreet gentleman," wrote such a "handsome serious" letter as reconciled the mother to her daughter, and she ever after treated her more as a friend than a child.

The next personage introduced into the narrative is Elizabeth Countess of Banbury, a sister of Lord Howard of Escrick. " My Lord Howard thought she was the fittest person to divert his son from his amour;" and the Countess, "who gloried much of her wit and contrivance," undertook the task to oblige her brother, and also (it is suggested) in order to induce him to further a projected marriage for her own son. On the 13th Feb. 1645-6, the Countess of Banbury arrived from France, bringing Mr. Howard with her. She had cajoled him to believe that she would forward his suit to Mistress Murray, but the result was that he shortly after formed an alliance with Lady Elizabeth Mordaunt, daughter of the Earl of Peterborough, which was privately solemnized in July 1646 (p. 18).

After her mother's death, Anne Murray was invited by her elder brother Charles and his lady to live with them, where she had an apartment for herself and her maid, and there stayed about a year.[a]

The next existing leaf of the narrative is lost, and we are abruptly introduced (p. 19) to Colonel Bamfield, a busy partisan of the royal family, who for some years after materially influenced the fortunes of the authoress. By his intervention she undertook

[a] Life, 1701, p. 15.

to contribute to the escape of the Duke of York from St. James's Palace, where that prince was detained in the custody of the Earl of Northumberland. Lady Halkett gives a very interesting relation how she provided a female dress for the Duke of York's disguise, how she dressed him, and he " was very pretty in it," (p. 22), and then dispatched him with a Wood-street cake, which she knew he loved. After some difficulties the Duke was safely lodged in a ship at Gravesend, when the lady of Colonel Washington assisted in his concealment, and his escape to the continent was effected.

Our authoress has a good deal more to say of Colonel Bamfield, for she soon began to entertain an interest in him, not only on account of his zealous efforts for the King's service, but also for his personal qualities. At an early stage of their intercourse she ventured to take him to task (p. 19) that he had not seen his wife for a twelvemonth; but he excused himself with the explanation that his wife lived amongst her own friends, who had declared for the Parliament, and therefore, though kind to her, were not well disposed towards him, and that their separation was necessary from prudential reasons during the existing state of public discord.

Some time after the Duke of York's escape, a report arrived that the Colonel's wife was dead (p. 25), and it was not long before he made an offer of his hand to Mistress Anne Murray : alleging that, should it please God to restore the King, he had a promise to be one of his Majesty's bedchamber, and their joint fortunes would amount to 800l. per annum. His frequent urging of this suit at last prevailed, and she promised to marry him as soon as it might prove convenient. It was shortly before the " murder " of the King that they arrived at this understanding. After that event, on Mistress Murray one day visiting the Colonel, she found him oppressed with extraordinary melancholy (p. 26), and, when she inquired the cause, she learned it was because news had been brought him that his wife was still living ! Unwilling to credit this report, he sent a trusty servant to ascertain the truth; who returned with an answer that her death had actually occurred at the time he heard of it, and that the messenger had seen her grave. Upon this, Anne Murray continued her former resolution to marry the Colonel, waiting only to take precautions against the sequestration of their property (p. 27).

About the same time her brother, Will Murray, came home from Court, much discontented. He had met with enemies among his associates, who accused him of keeping up a correspondence with Colonel Bamfield, in order to have the Duke of York crowned king in Scotland. Our author adds, that King Charles, though he did not believe the charge, was constrained to banish Will Murray from Court, sacrificing him to other persons whom he was afraid to offend. Landing at Gravesend, the discarded courtier was entertained at Cobham by the Duke and Duchess of Richmond; but almost immediately fell there into an illness from which he never recovered. An account of his deathbed, upon which he was attended by Dr. Wild, is given at some length (p. 29). He closed his life with the asseveration that, "Were I to live a thousand years, I would never set my foot in a Court again; for there is nothing in it but flattery and falsehood." It is afterwards mentioned that he was buried in the church of the Savoy, near his father and mother (p. 30).

After this sad occurrence, the author stayed for some time with her surviving brother, Charles Murray; but she was then prevailed upon to accept an invitation from Lady Howard to go home with her into the North. This lady was a daughter of Lord Howard of Escrick, and the same (to all appearance) whom our author first mentioned as the intimate friend of her early youth. Anne Howard had married her cousin Sir Charles Howard of Naworth Castle, afterwards the first Earl of Carlisle, a man of superior talents as well as station, and who seems to have been deservedly characterised as " one of the finest gentlemen."

It was on the 10th of September, 1649,[a] that the party commenced their journey, in which nothing disagreeable occurred until they arrived at Hinderskelfe, beyond York, a house belonging to Sir Charles Howard, and which was then occupied by his sisters. Whilst there, both Sir Charles and his lady had a severe fit of sickness; and afterwards their son, then about three years old, was attacked by the small-pox. His cure was attributed to the treatment of " Sir Thomas Gore, who studied physic more for divertisement than gain;" and there can be little doubt that this was Sir Thomas Gower of Stittenham, a brother-in-law of Sir Charles Howard, and lineal ancestor of the Duke of Sutherland, for no regular physician or other person of that name is on record as having lived at that period.

With reviving health the travellers proceeded to Naworth Castle in Cumberland, and a very interesting account is given of the well-governed household which was then maintained there (p. 31). Amongst the rest, the highest praise is accorded to the chaplain, Mr. Nicolls, with whose personal conduct towards herself our memorialist had afterwards great cause to be offended.

Whilst thus living in peace and contentment, the post, which passed one day in the week, brought sad intelligence. Colonel Bamfield, who had been preparing to follow her to the North, had been arrested and committed to the Gatehouse at Westminster, where he lay in danger of his life. To add to her distress, she soon after received letters, both from her brother Murray and her

---

[a] This date of the year is placed in the margin of the original MS. but was omitted by the transcriber.

sister Newton, declaring that they were convinced she had been deceived by Colonel Bamfield, for they were assured that his wife was still living, upon the authority of her uncle Sir Ralph S.[a]

Overcome by her feelings, Mistress Murray fell into a serious illness, in which she despaired of life (p. 32). She was unable to procure the attendance of a physician, but at length she was roused by Mrs. Culcheth, the wife of the house steward, to exert her own medical knowledge, which, " with the use of some cordialls," led to her recovery (p. 33).

Her prayers for Colonel Bamfield were soon after answered by the happy news that he had effected his escape from the Gatehouse, of the manner of which she gives a description (p. 34).

She next enters upon a detail of the treacherous method in which Mr. Nicolls, the chaplain at Naworth Castle, attempted to undermine her credit in the family. He asserted, on the suggested authority of Mr. Culcheth, the steward, that Lady Howard was jealous of Mistress Murray (p. 36), and he succeeded so far, by what he whispered in turn to either party, as to create a certain distrust and estrangement between the ladies. Mistress Murray was resolved to obtain an explanation, and she sought a private interview with Sir Charles Howard for that purpose (p. 38).

In the meantime, the Lady Howard had taken some objection to the chaplain's conduct towards two other young ladies who were resident in the family. They were sisters, " who had been bred up Papists, and by Sir Charles's example and care had become Protestants." The chaplain was employed for their instruction; but he was observed both by their waiting-woman and by Lady Howard herself to fondle the elder sister more kindly than was consistent with his usual gravity (p. 41). The circumstance of Lady Howard consulting our author on this delicate subject gave her an oppor-

---

[a] Shafto (?) of Benwill (?).

tunity to require an explanation of the grievance she herself experienced in the neglect of her old friend. This led to an *eclaircissement,* which proved, to the conviction of both the ladies, that the chaplain had acted a very double part (p. 45). At the same time it would seem that Mr. Nicolls fulfilled his joint functions of chaplain and secretary so usefully that he could not well be spared from the household at Naworth Castle.

Under these circumstances, Anne Murray determined to relinquish the hospitality of her old friends (p. 52). A letter from her sister Lady Newton communicated to her the fact that Sir Henry Newton, having accidentally met Colonel Bamfield on a passage to Flanders, had challenged him, and they fought soon after landing (p. 53). Their seconds were two colonels in the King's army. The name of her brother Newton's second she did not remember; but Bamfield's second was Colonel Loe, who afterwards came into Scotland with the King.

Sir Henry Newton was wounded in the hand, and the combatants were then parted; Colonel Bamfield throughout the affair lamenting that the voice of honour summoned him to use his sword against the brother of one whom he loved beyond any living person.

Whilst in Flanders, Colonel Bamfield had an opportunity of conversing with the Earl of Dunfermline, and of representing to his lordship both the state of his own affairs and the position of his friend Mistress Murray. He interested that nobleman in the favour of both parties. Lord Dunfermline was one of the Commissioners sent to invite the King to Scotland, and he showed his regard towards our author by writing to her with an assurance that if she came to Scotland she would there find many friends willing to assist her in recovering that portion of her inheritance which was in Scotch hands (p. 54). " The Earl of Dunfermline's concern in her was, that her mother had been educated in his father's family, and she, in duty and gratitude, had made his Lordship welcome to her house [in London] at all times when he came to Court." [a]

Her friends Sir Charles and Lady Howard very kindly seconded her wishes to proceed to Scotland (p. 54) They supplied her with money, and Sir Charles appointed an old gentleman, a kinsman of his own, to attend her to Edinburgh. After two days' journey she arrived in that city on the 6th of June, 1650. She took up her lodging at Sanders Peers', at the foot of the Canongate, where the mistress of the house soon recognised her as a sister of the late Will Murray, for both [he and she] had noticed the resemblance which the landlady bore to their deceased mother. By this means she was immediately put into communication with her mother's executor (p. 56).

She had not long to wait before she received a welcome recognition from the most influential leaders of the Royalist party. One of the first was the Earl of Argyle, who, having paid her a visit, sent his own coach for her in order that she might be received by his lady and her daughter Lady Anne Campbell. Their demeanour at once dissipated some of the prejudices she had hitherto entertained against Scotland. The Lady Anne " was very handsome, extremely obliging, and her behaviour and dress were equal to any she had seen in the Court of England;" and, when introduced to the Countess, she at once perceived whence her daughter had derived both her beauty and her " civility " or courtly polish. The former was now under some decay, but the latter " was so evident and so well-proportioned, that while she gave to others she reserved what was due to herself" (p. 57).

Only a few days after, Mistress Murray received and accepted from Sir James Douglas, who was brother to the Countess of Dunferm-

[a] Life. 1701, p. 22.

line, an invitation to stay with him and his lady at Aberdour. On the 15th of June she crossed from Leith to Burntisland, and on her landing Sir James Douglas took her by one hand and the Laird of Maines by the other, and bid her welcome to Fife. At that moment she stumbled and fell flat on the ground. Amidst the mutual apologies of her cavaliers she exclaimed, " I thinke I am going to take possession of itt!" but she often looked back to this accident as a presage of the blessings she was afterwards to enjoy in Fife, for there she eventually found a husband and a home.

It is an interesting notice of the attention which was even then paid by Scotchmen to horticulture, that, when conducted through the garden at Aberdour, she found it so fragrant and delightful that she could imagine she was still in England.

Lady Halkett very briefly notices a journey she made into Morayshire in June 1652 (p. 71) ; and thus describes the preparations she made for returning to Edinburgh. After an affectionate leave-taking of her friends in Lord Dunfermline's family, and of Mr. George Sharpe, the minister of Fyvie, she left that place on the 24th June, 1652, in company with the Earl, his nephew Lord Lyon, and other gentlemen.

Having arrived at Edinburgh, she went first to her former lodgings in the Canongate, and then to others at the Nether Bow, where one night when writing a letter her privacy was violently invaded by a patrol of the English soldiers; but through the interference of William Murray of Hermiston, " who was very great with the English officers," she exacted an apology.

To avoid the like intrusions in future, she was very glad to accept of some rooms in the house of the Earl of Tweeddale, for which the Countess of Balcarres, with equal kindness, provided furniture (p. 75).

She was now able to prosecute her law business. She began a

suit against the executors of Arthur Hay, who had been caution with the Earl of Kinnoull for a sum of £2,000 assigned to her by her late mother. The Lord Newbeth and his father gratuitously gave her their counsel.

At this time an accident made her acquainted with Sir James Halkett of Pitferran, her future husband. He was first brought to her lodging by the Earl of Dunfermline, on their way to the funeral of the lady of Sir John Gilmour.

It was on the [24th of June] that the King landed at [the mouth of the Spey].

When this important event became known to Mistress Murray, and she had reason to expect that his Majesty would soon turn his steps southwards, she began to fear what her reception might be, both on account of the disgrace of her late brother Will and of her own misfortune in the unhappy report that the wife of Colonel Bamfield was still alive. In order to feel her way she wrote to Mr. Henry Seymour, who was one of the grooms of the King's bedchamber, and had been a fellow-servant of her brother Charles. His answer, dated from Falkland on the 17th June, 1650 (and which is given in p. 58) assured her that the King gave no credit to the false rumours with which the world was then too full.

Soon after, accompanying Sir James Douglas, she repaired to the palace of Dunfermline, which they reached some three hours before the King's arrival (p. 59). In company with the Countess of Dunfermline and the Lady Anne Erskine she was introduced into the King's presence by the Marquess of Argyle and other persons of honour, and the ladies kissed his Majesty's hand. During the eight or ten subsequent days during which the King was entertained at Dunfermline those ladies daily attended upon him at dinner or supper ; but Anne Murray was vexed that she obtained no special recognition from his Majesty. At last she solicited

Mr. Harding, one of the King's oldest servants, to remind him of her claims upon his notice; which the good old gentleman undertook to do; and the next day before Charles left the place he amended his manners by addressing to her a very gracious speech, in which he fully acknowledged the service she had performed in contributing to the Duke of York's escape (p. 60).

The reader is next reminded of the confident anticipations of success which the royal party entertained before the Battle of Dunbar, and the complete dash to its hopes by the triumph of Cromwell in that struggle.

There was no alternative to the Earl of Dunfermline and his friends but to retreat further north. The Countess kindly invited Mistress Murray to share her reduced fortunes, and on the 7th of September they left Dunfermline.

On their road to Kinross they passed many of the wounded soldiers who were still straggling from the late battle. Anne Murray was the Miss Nightingale of that time. She invited them to come to her to the Countess's lodging at Kinross, where during the next two days at least three score were attended by herself and her woman, with the assistance of a man—perhaps not actually a surgeon—named Ar. Ro. for those patients whose wounds were such as were unfit for her treatment.

On the Monday she continued her journey with the Countess of Dunfermline to St. Johnstoon or Perth, where the King and Court then were. There also they found the Countess of Kinnoull, Lady Argyle's sister, at whose house the Lord Lorne, the Marquess of Argyle's son, came, and told her, at first with some mystery, that her name had been frequently that day before the council. He presently explained that her good deeds to the wounded soldiers had been favourably reported, and that the King was pleased to give her thanks for her charity, at the same time recognising the necessity that hospitals and surgeons should be established in several towns, to which the wounded might resort.

On the 19th of September the Countess of Dunfermline, with the author in her company, left Perth, in order to proceed to Fyvie, her husband's castle in Aberdeenshire. The journey, during which two nights were passed at Brechin and four at Aberdeen, lasted to the 27th of the month (p. 64).

Some time after, the King came to Aberdeen, where, being presented by some of his loyal subjects with a purse of gold, he was pleased to assign fifty pieces to Mistress Murray, in performance of his promise to acknowledge her services to the wounded soldiers. This enabled her to repay 25l. which earlier in the year she had borrowed of Sir George S——.

While at Fyvie Mistress Murray received a letter from Colonel B[amfield], requesting permission to visit her. He came after some delay, and found her much weakened from another attack of illness. It was still a question whether his wife was living; but he was desirous to make the most solemn asseverations that he believed the contrary to be the fact. He stayed for two days.[a]

She remained for nearly two years at Fyvie, in the greatest contentment, her most important occupation being the care of the sick and wounded persons, of whose cases she describes some of the most remarkable (p. 66).

When the King marched into England, the Earl of Dunfermline was one of the council left behind for the government of Scotland; but the ill-success of the royal forces at Worcester soon terminated this state of affairs. His lordship then retired from Edinburgh to Fyvie; and, when the army of the Parliament arrived at Aberdeen, he retired still further into Moray until he could arrange terms of capitulation.

---

[a] Mr. Nichols had written "this was the last time that Anne Murray saw him." But see the next page.

Some of the English soldiers at length found their way to Fyvie, and spread terror in a household consisting chiefly of women and children. Mistress Murray was requested by the Countess of Dunfermline to parley with their leader, and she did so, as she tells us, with a successful result (p. 68).

Some time after, three entire regiments arrived at Fyvie Castle. They were commanded by Colonel Lilburne, Colonel Fitz, and Colonel Overton. The second of these, Colonel Fitz, was recognised by Mistress Murray as an old acquaintance at Naworth Castle. With Colonel Overton she had a remarkable conversation, very consistent with the known character of the man.

Shortly after, Mistress Murray determined to go to England and revisit her old friend Lady Howard at Naworth Castle. On her way she stayed two or three days with the Countess of Roxburgh at Fleurs, and afterwards met Colonel Bamfield by appointment at Alnwick. He dissuaded her from returning to Naworth, because there were some persons there she was not desirous to meet. Having sent her servant for the trunks she had left there, she returned to Edinburgh.

The lady of Sir Robert Moray, expecting to give birth to a child, desired some rooms in Lord Tweeddale's house, and our author derived much pleasure from her society. Sir James Halkett, who was cousin-german to Sir Robert Moray, was at the same time a frequent visitor; and Anne Murray, divining his sentiments, sought an opportunity to disclose to him that she considered herself irrevocably engaged to Colonel Bamfield. Sir James Halkett received the disclosure with surprise, but at the same time with kindness, and was desirous to serve the colonel to the utmost of his power.

Colonel Bamfield now came to Edinburgh and joined a cabal of Royalists, who met every night in Lord Tweeddale's house. Among those who came most frequently were the Earl of Dunfermline, Lord Balcarres, Sir James Halkett, and Sir George Mackenzie of Tarbet.

The Christmas of 1652 was attended by some ominous incidents. An English woman, who " kept a change" or ordinary, and had been a servant of Lady Balcarres, having, in accordance with the English custom, prepared a dish of minced pies, brought two of them as an offering, saying that one was intended for Sir Robert Moray and his wife, the other for Sir James Halkett and Mistress Murray. This raised a general smile, except on the face of Mistress Murray herself. However, all were extremely merry. But a woman named Jane Hamilton, reported to possess the gift of second sight, remarked, " There is a great deal of mirth in this house to-day, but before this day eight days there will be as much sadness." This was verified by the very painful death of Lady Moray, whose strength was not sufficient to give birth to her expected child.

On the 6th February, 1652-3, Colonel Bamfield took his leave, having arranged to go to the North of Scotland to raise a force for the King's reception. Jane Hamilton again uttered one of her prophecies, declaring that the Colonel would never become Anne Murray's husband.

Mistress Murray now left the Earl of Tweeddale's house for a lodging at the foot of Blackfriars Wynd ; and soon after the Earl of Roxburgh, returning from London, brought from her sister an affectionate letter and the very acceptable present of 20*l.*

Sir James Halkett's attentions to her were persevering, but, from her previous engagement, unacceptable. To divert his attention she endeavoured to persuade him to marry, and even undertook to write to Lord Balcarres in order to forward his interest with a rich young widow. This suggests the introduction of an anecdote relative to the conduct of Sir James Halkett in the attack made upon Musselburgh. It appears that some reflections had been made upon his conduct on that occasion. Lord Balcarres relates that the King had been a witness of the whole affair from the leads of

Lord Balmerino's house at Leith, and had frequently given testimony to his good conduct (p. 84).

It was on the 21st of March, 1652-53, that Sir James Halkett was to go to Balcarres upon his matrimonial project; and that very day he heard from Colonel Hay that the wife of Colonel Bamfield was undoubtedly living. Just on the arrival of this overwhelming intelligence, another hiatus in the MS. occurs.

In May, 1653, the Earl of Dunfermline came to Mistress Murray, and, telling her that he had obtained information that measures would be taken to arrest the Earl of Balcarres upon the next day, requested her to undertake the task of warning that nobleman of his danger, as she was the only person he could trust. Upon this dangerous service she entered with her characteristic energy, and successfully accomplished it.

But the toil and excitement immediately brought on a serious illness, which kept her for some time at Balcarres. She could not have the aid of Dr. Cunningham, because he was gone with Lord Balcarres, and no other physician could be procured. She had frequent visits from ladies in the neighbourhood, particularly the Lady Ardross; and Mr. D. Forsyth and Mr. H. Rymer, apparently two ministers, paid her daily attention. On her recovery, after staying a week at the house of Lady Ardross, she returned to Edinburgh.

Sir James Halkett now urged his suit more warmly, but she declared that she was resolved not to marry at all (p. 89). However, she did not prohibit the continuance of his intercourse with her, and soon after she complied with his request that she would take charge of his two daughters. The younger was then but a child; but the elder near a woman, " and even then by more than ordinary discretion gave expectation of what she subsequently made good."

Upon this occasion Mistress Murray removed from the foot to the head of Blackfriars Wynd. She there resided with much content at one Mr. Glover's, Sir James Halkett coming often to see his children, and often bringing their uncle Sir Robert Montgomery and their cousin Haslehead.

Sir James Halkett again urged his suit, and summoned Mr. David Dickson, the minister of   , to his aid. Mistress Murray unfolded her tale to that worthy man, " not doubting but that he would resolve the question upon her side of the argument; but, after listening with much attention and sympathy, he took the opposite view, telling her that not only was she released by what had occurred from any engagement she had made to Colonel Bam-field, but that she might even be guilty of a fault if she neglected the offer of Sir James Halkett (p. 92). At length, after further discussion, she gave a conditional promise to Sir James, dependent upon the settlement of her pecuniary affairs, and the assistance of her brother in that respect (p. 93).

Soon after, Sir James Halkett went to London to assist the Countess of Morton (then a widow) in some important business, and he returned to Mistress Murray with a kind message from her sister Lady Newton, and encouraging letters from others of her old friends.

This determined her to go to London herself, but she could not take her journey before the beginning of September 1654, when the old Countess of Dunfermline, having first taken her on a visit to Pinckie, provided her with the seasonable loan of ten pounds.

On the first night of her journey she rested at Cavers, the house of Sir James Halkett's sister. Sir James left his elder daughter there, (the younger being placed in a school at Edinburgh), and accompanied our traveller for one day longer. She then proceeded with her women, and a footman whom Sir James had promised to Lady

Newton. Of this footman she gives a remarkable account (p. 95). After riding for some days on horseback, she at last met the post-coach, in which she proceeded southwards. Its only occupants were Sir   Widdrington and his nephew Mr. Errington, their man-servant, herself, and her woman. Though she was travelling under a borrowed name, her companions (who were Roman Catholics) discovered who she was, upon her mentioning the name of Mr. Fallowfield, an old priest that used sometimes to recommend sick persons to her care when at Naworth Castle (p. 96).

After arriving at Highgate one day at two in the afternoon, she sent the footman on to London, directing him to provide her a lodging, and bring a coach for her the next morning. She went to Whitefriars, where her brother Newton's lodging used to be, and where she would enjoy some immunity if her London creditors were inclined to be troublesome. She then wrote to her sister, who was at that time at Warwick.

[Lady Halkett's creditors did not press hardly upon her. Her brother-in-law, Sir Henry Newton, lent her 300*l*. and the Countess of Devonshire lent her 200*l*. As soon as she had settled her affairs she was in a position to listen to Sir James's offers, and, after a day set " apart solemnly by fasting and prayer to beg God's direction in an affair of so great importance," she accepted him as her future husband. They were married on March 2, 1656, in her brother-in-law Newton's closet, by Mr. Gaile, chaplain to the Countess of Devonshire, whom they had brought from London to Charleton for that end. After a few days they took leave of their friends and set out for Scotland in the post-coach.

Sir James was a widower with two sons and two daughters, and he had also four children by this his second wife, all of whom " died " except Robert.

When the Restoration came, she had, like many others, pleas to urge for the repayment of money advanced to the Crown or spent in its interest. Like most others, she failed to obtain any satisfaction for her demands. " All she gained was to learn not to confide in anyone upon earth."

Her married life was a happy one. But her husband died in 1676; and she outlived him, a sorrowing widow, till 1699. She left behind her a large collection of devotional meditations, of which one upon the 25th Psalm was published at Edinburgh in 1778, together with a sketch of her life.]

THE AUTOBIOGRAPHY

OF

ANNE LADY HALKETT.

AUTOBIOGRAPHY

OF

ANNE LADY HALKETT.

ᵃFor my parents I need nott say much, since they were well [known], and I need not bee ashamed to owne them by * *. It was mentioned as my reproach that I was of [mean extract]ion ; whereas hee that now succeds to that fa[milly] * * was once, was as good a Gentleman as any. [For that ma[tter] I shall ever be sattisfied with what can [be said to] the advanttage of that familly ; but some that [I am akin] to, both by father and mother, would take itt ill not [to be] thought Gentlemen, for my father claimed the honor of being derived from the Earle of Tillibardin's familly, and my mother from the Earle of Perth's.

Hee was thought a wise King who made choice of my father to bee tutor to the late King of blesed memory; and what that excellent Prince learnt in his youth kept him Stedfast in his relligion, though under all the temptations of Spaine, Temperate in all the exceses that attend a Court, Vertuous and Constant to the only lawfull embraces of the Queene, and unmoveable and undisturbed under all his unparalleld sufferings. For a recompense to my father's care in discharging his duty, hee was made Provost of Eaton Col-

---

* The first leaf of the MS. (pp. 3 and 4) is very much mutilated. After some pious introductory remarks regarding patience under affliction, the writer begins her narrative as above, the words in [ ] being supplied where the paper is either torn or worn.

ledge; where hee staid not long, but died when I was but three
months old,—yett it seemes the short time he lived amongst those
prebends they were so well satisfied, both with him and my mother,
that after my father's death they petitioned to have his place continued to my mother a yeare, which was never before granted to any
woman; and during her time they all renued their leases, as a testimony of their respect and desire to give her that advantage.

As this may evidence what my father's partes were, so my mother
may be best knowne by beeing thought fitt, both by the late King
and Queenes Majesty, to be entrusted twice with the charge and
honor of beeing Governese to the Duke of Glocester and the
Princese Elizabeth; the first during the time that the Countese of
Roxbery (who owned my mother for her cousin) went and continued in Holland with the Princese Royall; and then again
when my Lady Roxbery died. The first was only by a verball
order; butt the last was under the signett, dated (*blank*), wch I
have by mee to produce if itt were nesesary.

By this short account I have given of my parents it will be seen
what trust the greatest thought them cap[able of], wherfore they
could not butt performe a duty to [their children], butt that care was
wholy left (next to God's providence) to my mother,—my father
dying when wee were all very young,—who spared noe expence in
educating all her children in the most suitable way to improve them,
and if I made not the advantage I might have done it was my own
fault, and not my mother's, who paid masters for teaching my sister
and mee to write, speake French, play on the lute and virginalls, and
dance, and kept a gentlewoman to teach us all kinds of needleworke,
which shews I was not brought up in an idle life. But my mother's
greatest care, and for which I shall ever owne to her memory the
highest gratitude, was the great care she tooke that, even from our
infancy, wee were instructed never to neglect to begin and end the
day with prayer, and orderly every morning to read the Bible, and
ever to keepe the church as offten as there was occation to meet
there, either for prayers or preaching. So that for many yeares

together I was seldome or never absent from divine service, at five a' clocke in the morning in the summer, and sixe a' clocke in the winter, till the usurped power putt a restraint to that puplicke worship so long owned and continued in the Church of England; where, I blese God, I had my education, and the example of a good Mother, who kept constantt to her owne parish church, and had allways a great respect for the ministers under whose charge shee was.

What my childish actions were I thinke I need not give accountt of here, for I hope none will thinke they could bee either vicious or scandalous. And from that time till the year 1644 I may truly say all my converse was so inocentt that my owne hart cannott challenge mee with any imodesty, either in thought or behavier, or an act of disobedience to my mother, to whom I was so observant that as long as shee lived I doe nott remember that I made a visitt to y⁰ neerest neibour or wentt anywhere withoutt her liberty. And so scrupulous I was of giving any occation to speake of mee, as I know they did of others, that though I loved well to see plays and to walke in the Spring Garden sometimes (before itt grew something scandalous by y⁰ abuse of some), yett I cannott remember 3 times that ever I wentt with any man besides my brothers; and if I did, my sisters or others better than my selfe was with mee. And I was the first that proposed and practised itt, for 3 or 4 of us going together withoutt any man, and every one paying for themselves by giving the mony to the footman who waited on us, and he gave itt in the play-howse. And this I did first upon hearing some gentlemen telling what ladys they had waited on to plays, and how much itt had cost them; upon which I resolved none should say the same of mee.

In the yeare 1644 I confese I was guilty of an act of disobedience, for I gave way to y⁰ adrese of a person whom my mother, att the first time that ever hee had occation to bee conversantt wᵗʰ mee, had absolutely discharged mee ever to allow of: And though before ever I saw him severalls did tell mee that there would bee something more than ordinary betwixt him and mee (wᶜʰ I believe they fudged from the great friendship betwixt his sister and mee, for wee were seldome assunder att London, and shee and I were bedfellows when shee came to my sister's house att Charleton, where for ye most part shee staid while wee continued in the country,) yett he was halfe a yeare in my company before I discovered anything of a particular inclination for mee more than another; and, as I was civill to him both for his owne merit and his sister sake, so any particular civility I received from him I looked upon it as flowing from the affection hee had to his sister, and her kindness to mee. After that time, itt seemes hee was nott so much master of himselfe as to conceale itt any longer. And having never any opertunity of being alone with mee to speake himselfe, hee imployed a young gentleman (whose confidentt he was in an amour betwixt him and my Lady Anne his cousin-german,) to tell mee how much hee had indeavored all this time to smother his passion, which he said began the first time that ever hee saw mee, and now was come to that height that if I did nott give him some hopes of favor he was resolved to goe back againe into France (from whence he had come when I first saw him) and turn Capucin. Though this discourse disturbed mee, yett I was a weeke or ten days before I would be persuaded so much as to heare him speake of this subject, and desired his friend to representt severall disadvantages that itt would bee to him to pursue such a designe. And, knowing that his father had sentt for him outt of France with an intention to marry him to sum rich match that might improve his fortune, itt would be high ingratitude in mee to doe anything to hinder such a designe, since his father had beene so obliging to my mother and sister as to use his Lord^s interest with ye Parliamentt to preventt the ruine of my brother's howse and k[in ?] ; butt when all I could say to him by his friend could not prevaile, butt that hee grewe so ill and discontented that all the howse tooke notice, I did yield so farre to comply with his desire as to give him liberty one day when I was walking in ye gallery to come there and speake to mee. What he saide was handsome and short, butt much disordered, for hee

looked pale as death, and his hande trembled when he tooke mine
to lead mee, and with a great sigh said, " If I loved you lese I
could say more." I told him I could nott butt thinke myselfe
much obleeged to him for his good opinion of mee, butt itt would
be a higher obligation to confirme his esteeme of mee by following
my advice, which I should now give him my selfe, since hee would
not receave itt by his friend. I used many arguements to diswade
him from pursuing what hee proposed. And, in conclusion, told
him I was 2 or 3 yeare older than hee, and were there no other
objection, yett that was of such weight with mee as would never
lett mee allow his further adrese. " Madam, (said he,) what I
love in you may well increase, butt I am sure itt can never decay."
I left arguing, and told him I would advise him to consult with
his owne reason, and that would lett him see I had more respect
to him in denying than in granting what with so much passion
he desired.

After that hee sought, and I shunned, all opertunittys of private
discourse with him; butt one day, in ye garden, his friend tooke his
sister by the hand and lead her into another walke, and left him
and I together : and hee, with very much seriousnese, began to tell
mee that hee had observed ever since hee had discovered his affection to mee that I was more reserved and avoided all converse with
him, and therefore, since hee had no hopes of my faver, hee was
resolved to leave England, since he could not bee hapy in itt. And
that what ever became of him y^t might make him displease either
his father or his friends I was the occation of it, for if I would not
give him hopes of marying him hee was resolved to putt him selfe
outt of a capacity of marying any other, and go imediately into
a conventt. And that he had taken order to have post horses
ready against the next day. I confese this discourse disturbed mee,
for though I had had noe respect for him, his sister, or his family,
yett relligion was a tye upon mee to endeaver the prevention of the
hazard of his soule. I looked on this as a violent passion wch would
nott last long, and perhaps might grow the more by beeing resisted,

when as a seeming complaisance might lessen itt. I told him I was
sory to have him intertaine such thoughts as could nott butt bee a
ruine to him and a great affliction to all his relations, wch I would
willingly preventt if itt were in my power. He said itt was absolutely in my power, for if I would promise to marry him hee should
esteeme himselfe the most hapy man living, and hee would waite
what ever time I thought most convenientt for itt. I replied I
thought it was unreasonable to urge mee to promise that wch ere
long hee might repentt the asking; butt this I would promise to
sattisfy him, that I would not marry till I saw him first maried.
Hee kist my hand upon that with as much joy as if I had confirmed
to him his greatest hapinese, and said hee could desire noe more, for
hee was secure I should never see nor heare of that till itt was to
my selfe. Upon this wee parted both well pleased, for hee thought
hee had gained much in what I promised, and I looked upon my
promise as a cure to him, butt noe inconvenience to myself, since I
had noe inclination to marry any. And though I had, a delay in
itt was the least returne I could make to soe deserving a person.
Butt I deceaved myselfe by thinking this was the way to moderate
his passion, for now hee gave way to itt without any restraintt, and
thought himselfe soe secure of mee as if there had beene nothing to
opose itt, though hee managed itt with that discretion that it was
scarce visible to any within the howse; nott so much as either his
sister or mine had the least suspittion of it, for I had injoyned him
not to lett y^m or any other know what his designes were, because
I would not have them accesory, what ever fault might bee in the
prosecution of itt. Thus it continued till towards winter that his
sister was to goe home to her father againe, and then, knowing hee
would want much of the opertunity hee had to converse with mee,
hee was then very importunate to have mee consent to marry him
privately, wch itt scemes hee pleased himselfe so with the hopes of
prevailing with me that he had provided a wedding ring and a
minister to marry us. I was much unsattisfied with his going that
lengh, and, in short, told him hee need never expect I would marry

him without his father and my mother's consent; if that could be
obtained, I should willingly give him the sattisfaction hee desired,
butt withoutt that I could not expect God's blesing neither upon
him nor mee, and I would doe nothing that was so certaine a way
to bring ruine upon us both. Hee used many arguments from y^e
examples of others who had practised the same, and was hapy both
in their parents' faver and in one another, butt, finding mee fixt
beyond any persuasion, hee resolved to acquaintt my sister with itt,
and to imploy her to speake of itt to his father and my mother.
Shee very unwillingly undertooke it, because shee knew itt would be
a surprise to them, and very unwellcome. Butt his impertunity
prevailed, and shee first acquainted my mother with itt; who was so
pasionately offended with the proposall y^t, wheras his father might
have beene brought to have given his consentt (having ever had a
good opinion of mee and very civill), shee did so exasperate him
against itt, that nothing could sattisfy her but presently to putt itt
to Mr. H.'s choice either presently to marry a rich cittisen's daughter
that his father had designed for him, or els to leave England.

The reason I believe y^t made my mother the more incensed was,
first that itt was what in ye beginning of our aquaintance shee
had absolutely discharged my having a thought of allowing
such an adrese ; and though in some respect his quality was
above mine, and therefore better then any shee could expect
for mee, yett my Lord H.'s fortune was such as had need of a
more considerable portion then my mother could give mee, or els it
must ruine his younger chilldren, and therefore my mother would
not consentt to itt, though my Lord H. did offer to doe the uttmost
his condition would allow him if shee would lett me take my hazard
with his son. Butt my mother would nott bee persuaded to itt
upon noe consideration, lest any should have thought itt was begun
with her allowance; and to take away ye suspittion of that did, I
believe, make her the more violent in oposing itt, and the more
scavere to mee. My sister made choice of Sunday to speake of itt.
First, because shee thought that day might putt y^m both in a

calmer frame to heare her, and confine there passion, since it would bee the next day before they would determine anything. Butt finding both by my mother and my L. H. that they intended nothing butt to part us, so as never to meet againe, except it was as strangers, Mr. H. was very importunate to have an opertunity to speake with mee that night, wch I gave. My sister beeing only with mee, we came downe together to ye roome I apointed to meett with him. I confese I never saw those two pasions of love and regrett more truly represented, nor could any person expresse greater affection and resolution of constancy, wch with many solemne oaths hee scaled of never loving or marying any butt my selfe. I was not sattisfied with his swearing to future performances, since I said both hee and I might find itt most convenient to retract; but this I did assure him, as long as hee was constantt hee should never find a change in mee, for though duty did oblicege mee nott to marry any withoutt my mother's consentt, yett itt would nott tye mee to marry without my owne. My sister at this rises, and said, " I did nott thinke you would have ingaged me to be a wittnese of both your resolutions to continue what I expected you would rather have laid aside, and therefore I will leave you." " Oh, madam, (said hee,) can you imagine I love att that rate as to have itt shaken with any storme ? Noe ; were I secure your sister would not suffer in my absence by her mother's sevearity I would nott care what misery I were exposed to; butt to thinke I should bee ye occation of trouble to the person in ye earth that I love most is unsuportable ;" and with that hee fell downe in a chaire that was behind him, but as one without all sence, wch I must confese did so much move mee, y^t laing aside all former distance I had kept him att, I sat downe upon his knee, and laying my head neare his I suffred him to kisse mee, wch was a liberty I never gave before, nor had nott then had I nott scene him so overcome with griefe, wch I endeavered to supprese with all ye incouragement I could, butt still presing him to be obedientt to his father, either in going abroad or staying att home, as hee thought most convenient. " Noe, (says he,) since they will not allow mee to converse with you, France will bee more agreeable to mee then England, nor will I goe there except I have liberty to come here againe and take my leave of you." To that I could not disagree if they thought fitt to allow itt; and so my sister and I left him, butt she durst nott owne to my mother where shee had beene.

The next morning early my Lord H. went away, and tooke with him his son and daughter, and left me to the seaveritys of my offended mother, who nothing could pacify. Affter she had called for me, and said as many bitter things as passion could dictate upon such a subject, shee discharged mee to see him, and did solemnly vow that if shee should heare I did see Mr. H. shee would turne mee outt of her doores, and never owne mee againe. All I said to that part was that itt should be against my will if ever shee heard of itt. Upon Tuesday my Lord H. writt to my mother that hee had determined to send his son to France, and that upon Thursday after he was to begin his journy; butt all he desired before hee wentt was to have liberty to see mee, wch he thought was a sattisfaction could nott bee denyed him, and therefore desired my mother's consentt to itt; wch shee gave upon the condittion that hee should only come in and take his leave of mee, butt nott to have any converse but what shee should bee a wittnese of her selfe. This would nott att all please Mr. H., and therfore seemed to lay the desire of itt aside. In the meane time my chamber and liberty of lying alone was taken from mee, and my sister's woman was to bee my guardian, who watched sufficiently so that I had not the least opertunity either day or night to bee without her. Upon Thursday morning early my mother sentt a man of my sister's (whose name I must mention with ye rest that att that [time] was in the familly, for there was Moses, Aron, and Miriam all at one time in itt, and none either related or acquainted together till they mett there)— this Moses was sent to my Lord H. with a letter to inquire if his son were gone. I must here relate a little odd incounter wch agravated my misfortune. There came no returne till night, and

having gott liberty to walke in the hall my mother sent a child
of my sister's and bid him walke with mee, and keepe mee company. I had not beene there a quarter of an hower butt my maid
Miriam came to mee and told mee shee was walkeing at the backe
gate and Mr. H. came to her and sentt her to desire mee to come
there and speake butt two or three words with him, for hee had
sworne nott to goe away without seeing mee, nor would hee come
in to see my mother, for he had left London that morning very
early and had rod up and downe that part of the country only
till itt was ye gloome of ye evening to have the more privacy
in comming to see mee. I bid her goe back and tell him I
durst not see him because of my mother's oath and her discharge.
While shee was presing me to run to the gate, and I was neere to
take the start, the child cried outt, " O, my aunt is going ;" w^{ch}
stoped me, and I sent her away to tell ye reason why I could nott
come. I still staid walking in the hall till shee returned, wondring
shee staid so long. When shee came, shee was hardly able to
speake, and with great disorder said, " I believe you are ye most
unfortunate person living, for I thinke Mr. H. is killed." Any one
that hath ever knowne what gratitude was, may imagine how these
words disordered me; butt, impatientt to know how (I was resolved
to hazard my mother's displeasure rather then nott see him), shee
told me that while shee was telling him my answeare there came a
fellow with a great club behind him and strucke him downe dead,
and others had seazed upon Mr. T. (who formerly had beene his
governer, and was now intrusted to see him safe on ship boord,)
and his man. The reason of this was from what there was too
many sad examples of att that time when the devision was betwixt
ye King and Parliamentt, for to betray a master or a friend was
looked upon as doing God good service. My brother-in-law S^r
Henry Newton had beene long from home in attendance on the
King, for whose service hee had raised a troope of horse upon his
owne expence, and had upon all occations testified his loyalty, for
wch all his estate was sequestred, and with much dificulty my sister

gott liberty to live in her owne house, and had the fifth part to live upon, wch was obtained with impertunity. There was one of my brother's tenants called Musgrove, who was a very great rouge, who farmed my brother's land of ye Parliamentt, and was imployed by them as a spye to discover any of the Cavaliers that should come within his knowledge: hee, observing 3 gentlemen upon good horse scoutting about all day and keeping att a distance from the high way, aprehends itt was my brother who had come privately home to see my sister, and resolves to watch when hee came neere ye house, and had followed so close as to come behind and give Mr. H. that stroake, thinking itt had beene my brother Newton, and seased upon his governor and servantt (the post boy being left att some distance with the horses). In the midst of this disorder Moses came there, and Miriam having told what the occation of itt was, hee told Musgrove itt was my Lord H. son hee had used so ; upon which hee and his complices wentt imediately away, and Moses and Mr. H.'s man caried him into an alehouse hard by and laid him on a bed, where hee lay some time before hee came to himselfe. So, hearing all was quiett againe, and that hee had noe hurt, only stonished with the blow, I wentt into ye roome where I had left my mother and sister, wch being att a good distance from the backe gate they had heard nothing of the tumult y^t had been there. A litle after Moses came in and delivered a letter from my Lord Howard, wch affter my mother had read, she asked what news att London. Hee answeared, the greatest hee could tell was that Mr. H. wentt away that morning early post to Deepe, and was going to France, butt hee could nott learne the reason of it. My mother and sister seemed to wonder att itt, for none in the familly except my maid knew any thing that had fallen outt, or had any suspition I was concerned in itt, but my mother and sister. After Moses went out my mother asked mee if I was nott ashamed to thinke that it would be said my Lord H. was forced to send away his son to secure him from mee. I said I could not butt regrett whatever had occationed her displeasure or his punishmentt, butt I was guilty of noe unhandsome action to make mee ashamed, and therefore, whatever were my present misfortune, I was confidentt to evidence before I died that noe child shee had had greater love and respect to her or more obedience ; to wch shee replied, It seems you have a good opinion of yourselfe.

My mother now beleeving Mr. H. gone, I was nott as former nights sentt to my bed and ye guard upon mee that was usuall, butt I staid in my mother's chamber till shee and my sister (who lay together) was a'bed. In the meane time Mr. H. had sentt for Moses and told him what ever misfortune he might suffer by his stay there hee was fully determined nott to goe away without seeing mee, and desired I would come to the banketting howse in ye garden and hee would come to ye window and speake to mee ; wch he told mee, and with all that Mr. T. (who was a very serious good man) did earnestly intreat mee to condescend to his desire to preventt what might be more inconvenientt to us both. I sent him word when my mother was a'bed I would contrive some way to sattisfy him, butt nott where hee proposed, because it was within the view of my mother's chamber window. After I had left my mother and sister in there bed I wentt alone in the darke through my brother's closett to ye chamber where I lay, and as I entered the roome I laid my hand upon my eyes, and with a sad sigh said, Was ever creature so unfortunate and putt to such a sad deficulty, either to make Mr. H. forsworne if hee see mee nott, or if I doe see him my mother will bee foresworne if shee doth nott expose mee to the utmost rigour her anger can inventt! In the midst of this dispute with myselfe what I should doe, my hand beeing still upon my eyes, itt presently came in my mind that if I blindfolded my eyes that would secure mee from seeing him, and so I did not transgrese against my mother, and hee might that way satisfy himselfe by speaking with mee. I had as much joy in finding outt this meanes to yeeld to him without disquiett to my selfe as if itt had beene of more considerable consequence. Imediately I sentt Moses to tell him upon what condittions I would speake with him; first, that hee must allow mee to

have my eyes covered, and that hee should bring Mr. T. with him,
and if thus hee were sattisfied I ordered him to bring them in the
backe way into yᵉ cellar, where I with Miriam would meett them
the other way; wᶜʰ they did. As soon as Mr. H. saw mee hee much
importuned the taking away the covert from my eyes; wᶜʰ I not
suffering, hee left disputing that, to employ the litle time hee had in
regretting my nott yielding to his importunity to marry him before
his affection was discovered to his father and my mother, for had itt
beene once past there power to undoe, they would [have] beene sooner
sattisfied, and wee might have been hapy together and not indured
this sad separation. I told him I was sory for beeing the occation
of his discontentt, butt I could nott repentt the doing my duty
what ever ill successe itt had, for I ever looked upon marying
withoutt consentt of parentts as the highest act of ingratitude and
disobedience that chilldren could committ, and I resolved never to
bee guilty of itt. I found his greatest trouble was the feare hee
had that my mother in his absence would force me to marry M. L.
(who was a gentleman of a good fortune who some people thought
had a respect for mee). To this I gave him as much assurance as I
could that neither hee nor any other person liveing should lessen
his interest till hee gave mee reason for itt himselfe. Itt is un-
nesesary to repeatt the solemne oaths hee made never to love nor
marry any other, for, as I did nott aprove of itt then, so I will nott
now agravate his crime by mentioning them. Butt there was
nothing he left unsaid that could exprese a sinceare vertuous true
affection. Mr. T. (who with Moses and Miriam had all this time
beene so civill to us both as to retire att such a distance as nott to
heare what wee said,) came and interupted him, and desired him to
take his leave, lest longer stay might be prejudiciall to us all. I
called for a botlle of wine, and giving Mr. T. thankes for his civility
and care, drunk to him, wishing a good and hapy journey to Mr. H.
So taking a farewellᵃ of them both, I wentt up the way I came, and
left them to Moses' care to conduct them outt quiettly as hee led
them in.

ᵃ This was upon Thursday night yᵉ 10ᵗʰ of October, 1644.

This was not so secrettly done butt some of ye howse observed more noise than ordinarily used to bee att y^t time of night, and by sattisfying there curiosity in looking outt discovred the occation of itt; butt they were all so just as none of them ever aquainted my mother with itt, though I did not conceale itt from my sister the first opertunity I had to bee alone with her. I was in hopes, affter some time that Mr. H. was gone, my mother would have receaved mee into her faver againe, butt ye longer time shee had to consider of my fault the more shee did agravate itt. And though my Lord H. (who returned shortly affter with his daughter) and my sister did use all the argumentts imaginable to persuade her to bee reconciled to mee, yet nothing would prevaile, except I would solemly promise never to thinke more of Mr. H. and y^t I would marry another whom shee thought fitt to propose; to wch I beged her pardon, for till Mr. H. was first maried I was fully determined to marry noe person living. Shee asked mee if I was such a foole as to believe he would be constantt. I said I did; but if he were nott, itt should bee his fault, nott mine, for I resolved nott to make him guilty by example. Many were employed to speake to mee. Some used good words, some ill; butt one that was most scavare, after I had heard her with much patience raile a long time, when she could say noe more I gave a true accountt how innocentt I was from having any design upon Mr. H. and related what I have allready mentioned of the progrese of his affection; which when she heard, shee sadly wept and beged my pardon, and promised to doe mee all the service shee could; and I beleeve shee did, for shee had much influence upon my Lord H. (having beene with his lady from a child), and did give so good a caracter of mee and my proceedings in that affaire with his son, that hee againe made an offer to my mother to send for his son if shee would consentt to the mariage; butt shee would nott heare itt spoken of, butt said shee rather I were buried than bring so much ruine to the familly shee honored. My mother's anger against mee increased to that height, that for fourteene months shee never gave me her blesing, nor never spoke to mee but when itt was to reproach mee; and one day said with much bitternese shee did hate to see mee. That word, I confese, strucke deepely to my hart, and putt mee to my thoughts what way to dispose of myselfe to free my mother from such an object. Affter many debates with my selfe, and inquirys what life I could take to that was most inocentt, I resolved and writt to Sr Patrick Drumond, a cousin of my mother's, who was Conservator in Holland, to doe mee the favor to informe mee if itt was true that I had heard that there was a nunery in Holland for those of the Protestant relligion, and that hee would inquire upon what condittions they admitted any to there society, because if they were consistent with my relligion I did resolve upon his advertisement imediately to goe over; and desired him to hasten an answeare, and not devulge to any what I had writt to him. About a fortnight after my mother sent for mee one morning into her chamber, and examined mee what I had writt to Sr Patrick Drumond. I ingeniously gave her an accountt, and ye reason of itt, for since I found nothing would please her that I could doe I was resolved to goe where I could most please my selfe, wch was in a solitary retired life, and so free her from the sight shee hated, and since itt was upon that consideration I did nott doubt the obtaining her consentt. It seemes Sr Patrick Drumond, who was a wise and honest gentleman, aprehending discontentt had made mee take that resolution wch I had writt to him about, instead of answearing my letter, writtes to my mother a very handsome serious letter, aquainting her with my intention, and concluded itt could proceed from nothing but her scavarity, perhaps upon unjust grounds, and therefore used many arguments to persuade her to returne to that wonted kindnese wch shee had ever shewed to all her chilldren, and what hee was sure I would deserve, what ever opinion shee had lately entertained to ye contrary. This hee presed with so much of reason and earnestnese that itt prevailed more with my mother than what ever had beene said before, and from that time she receaved mee againe to her favor, and ever affter used me more like a freind than a child. In the meane time all care was used that might preventt Mr H. corespondence and mine. Butt he found an excuse for sending home his man, beleeving him honest and faithfull to him, and with him hee writt and sentt me a presentt, butt instead of delivering them to mee gave them to his father, who otherwise disposed of them. Yett in requitall I sent backe with him a ring with five rubys, and gave him something for his paines, when hee came to me and indeavoured to vindicate himselfe by protesting y^t unexpectedly hee was searched as soone as ever hee entred his lord's house, and all was taken from him; butt I found afterwards hee was nott so honest as I beleeved, for hee never delivered my ring to his master, nor anything I intrusted him with.

Att this time my Lord H. had a sister in France, who gloried much of her witt and contrivance, and used to say shee never designed anything butt shee accomplished it. My Lord H. thought she was ye fittest person to divert his son from his amour, and to her hee writtes, and recommends itt to her managementt; who was nott neglegent of what shee was intrusted with, as apeared in the conclusion, though her cariage was a great disapointment to Mr H., for hee expected by her mediation to have obtained what he desired, and that made him the more willing to comply with her, who designed her own advantage by this to oblicge her brother, who might bee the more usefull to her in a projected mariage shee had for her owne son.

Upon Thursday ye 13. of February 1645-6, word was brought to my mother that ye Countese of B. was come outt of France, and Mr. H. with her, wch was a great surprise to her and all his relations. My mother examined mee if I had sentt for him, or knew any thing of his comming; wch I assured her I had nott, and shee said nott much more. Butt I was as much disturbed as any, sometimes thinking hee was come with an assurance from his auntt that shee would accomplish what he had so passionately desired, or els that hee had laid all thoughts of mee aside, and was come with a resolution to comply with his father's desires. The last opinion I was a litle confirmed in, having never receaved any word or

letter from him in ten days after his returne, and meeting him
accidentally where I was walking hee crosed the way, and another
time was in the roome when I came in to visitt some young ladys,
and neither of these times tooke any notice of mee more then of
one I had never seene. I confese I was a little disordered att itt,
butt made noe conclusions till I saw what time would produce.

Upon Tuesday the 4. of March, my Lady Anne W. his cousin came
to my mother's, and having staid a convenientt time for a visitt
with my mother (for then itt was nott usuall for mothers and
daughters to bee visited apart) I waited on her downe, and taking
mee aside, shee told mee shee was desired by her cousin T. H. to
presentt his most faithfull service to mee, and to desire mee nott to
take itt ill that hee did nott speake to me when hee mett mee, for
finding his auntt nott his friend as he expected hee seemed to comply with her desire only to have the opertunity of comming home
wth her, and had resolved for a time to forbeare all converse with
mee, and to make love to all that came in his way, butt assured mee
itt was only to make his friends think hee had forgott mee, and
then hee might with ye lese suspition prosecute his designe, wch was
never to love or marry any butt mee, and this shee said hee confirmed with all the solemne oaths imaginable. In pursuance of this
he visitted all the young ladys about the towne, butt an Earles
daughter gave him the most particular wellcome, whose mother not
allowing him to come as a pretender shee made apointmentt with
him and mett him att her cousin's howse frequently, wch I knew,
and hee made sport of. The summer being now advancing, my
mother and her familly wentt with my sister to her house in the
country; wch beeing nott farre from London, wee heard offten how
afaires wentt there, and amongst other discourse that it was reported
Mr. H. was in love with my Lady E. M. and shee with him, att
wch some smiled and said itt might bee her witt had taken him butt
certainly nott her beauty (for shee had as litle of that as my selfe).
Though these reports putt mee upon my guard yett I confese I did
not beleeve hee was reall in his adrese there, neither did his sister,

who was sometimes a wittnese of there converse and gave mee
accountt of itt; butt I aproved nott of his way, for I thought itt
could nott butt reflect upon him selfe, and injure either that lady
or mee. Butt shee tooke a way to secure her selfe; for upon the
last Tuesday in July 1646, a litle before super, I receaved a letter
from Mrs. H., a particular friend of mine, who writt mee word
that upon ye Tuesday before Mr. H. was privately maried to my
Lady E. M., and the relations of both sides was unsattisfied.

I was alone in my sister's chamber when I read the letter, and
flinging my selfe downe upon her bed, I said, " Is this the man for
whom I have sufred so much ?   Since hee hath made him selfe unworthy my love, hee is unworthy my anger or concerne;" and rising
imediately I wentt outt into the next roome to my super as uncon-
cernedly as if I had never had an interest in him, nor had never
lost itt.   A litle affter my mother came to the knowledge of itt
from my Lord H., who was much discontented att his son's mariage,
and offten wished hee had had his former choice. Nothing troubled
mee more than my mother's laughing att mee, and perhaps soe did
others, butt all I said was, " I thought hee had injured himself
more than mee, and I much rather hee had done itt then I;" and
once, I confese, in passion, being provoked by something I had
heard, I said with too much seriousnese, " I pray God hee may
never dye in peace till hee confese his fault, and aske mee forgive-
nese."   Butt I acknowledge this as a fault, and have a hundred
times beged the Lord's pardon for itt; for, though in some respects
itt might bee justified as wishing him repentance, yett many circumstances might make it imposible for mee to be a wittnese of itt.
And God forbid that any should wantt peace for my passion!
When Miriam first heard hee was maried shee lifted up her hands
and said, " Give her, O Lord, dry breasts, and a miscarying
wombe!" which I reproved her for; butt it seemes the Lord
thought fitt to grantt her request, for that lady miscaried of severall
chilldren before shee brought one to the full time, and that one
died presently after it was borne, wch may be a lesson to teach

people to governe there wishes and there toung, that neither may act to the prejudice of any, lest itt bee placed on there accountt att the day of reckoning. Nott only was this couple unfortunate in the chilldren, butt in one another, for itt was too well knowne how short a time continued the sattisfaction they had in one another. Nor did his aunt the Countese of *Banbery*, who first putt him

[*Pages* 24 *and* 25 *missing.*]

upon time and nott the worse that hee proffesed to have a grea friendship for my brother Will.

This gentleman came to see mee sometimes in the company ot ladys who had beene my mother's neibours in St Martin's Lane, and sometimes alone, butt when ever hee came his discourse was serious, handsome, and tending to imprese the advantages of piety, loyalty, and vertue; and these subjects were so agreeable to my owne inclination that I could nott butt give them a good reception, especially from one that seemed to bee so much an owner of them himselfe. Affter I had beene used to freedom of discourse with him I told him I aproved much of his advise to others, butt I thought his owne practise contradicted much of his proffesion, for one of his aquaintance had told mee hee had nott seene his wife in a twelvemonth, and itt was imposible, in my opinion, for a good man to bee an ill husband; and therefore hee must defend himselfe from one before I could beleeve the other of him. Hee said itt was not nesesary to give every one that might condemne him the reason of his being so long from her, yett to sattisfy mee hee would tell mee the truth, wch was, that hee beeing engaged in the King's service he was oblieged to bee att London, where itt was nott convenientt for her to bee with him, his stay in any place beeing uncertaine; besides, shee lived amongst her freinds, who, though they were kind to her, yett were nott so to him, for most of that country had declared for the Parleament, and were enemys to all that had or did serve the King, and therefore his wife, hee was sure, would not condemne him for what hee did by her owne consentt. This seeming reasonable, I did insist noe more upon that subject.

Att this time hee had frequentt letters from ye King, who imployed him in severall affaires, butt that of the greatest concerne wch hee was imployed in was to contrive the Duke of Yorke's escape outt of St James (where his Highnese and the Duke of Glocester and the Princese Elizabeth lived under the care of ye Earle of Northumberland and his lady). The dificultys of itt was represented by Coll. B.; but his Matie still pressed itt, and I remember this expresion was in one of the letters:—" I beleeve itt will bee deficult, and if hee miscary in the attempt itt will bee ye greatest afliction that can arive to mee; butt I looke upon James's escape as Charles's preservation, and nothing can content mee more; therfore bee carefull what you doe."

This letter, amongst others, hee showed mee, and where the King aproved of his choice of mee to intrust with itt, for to gett the Duke's cloaths made, and to drese him in his disguise. So now all C. B.'s busynese and care was how to manage this busynese of so important concerne, wch could not bee performed without severall persons' concurrence in itt, for hee beeing generally knowne as one whose stay att London was in order to serve the King, few of those who were intrusted by the Parliament in puplicke concernes durst owne convearse or hardly civility to him, lest they should have beene suspect by there party, wch made itt deficult for him to gett accese to ye Duke; but (to be short) having comunicated ye designe to a gentleman attending his Highnese, who was full of honor and fidelity, by his meanes hee had private accese to the Duke, to whom hee presented the King's letter and order to his Highnese for consenting to act what C. B. should contrive for his escape, wch was so cheerfully intertained and so readily obayed, that being once designed there was nothing more to doe than to prepare all things for the execution. I had desired him to take a ribban with him and bring mee the bignese of the Duke's wast and his lengh, to have cloaths made fitt for him. In the meane time C. B. was to provide mony for all nesesary expence, wch was furnished by an honest cittisen. When I gave the measure to my tailor to inquire how much mohaire would serve to make a petticoate and wastcoate to a young gentlewoman of that bignese and stature, hee considered itt a long time, and said hee had made many gownes and suites, butt hee had never made any to such a person in his life. I thought hee was in the right; butt his meaning was, hee had never seene any woman of so low a stature have so big a wast; however hee made itt as exactly fitt as if hee had taken the measure himselfe. Itt was a mixed mohaire of a light haire couler and blacke, and ye under-petticoate was scarlett.

All things beeing now ready, upon the 20. of Aprill, 1648, in the evening, was the time resolved on for ye Duke's escape. And in order to that, itt was designed for a week before every night as soon as ye Duke had suped hee and those servants that attended his Highnese (till the Earle of Northumberland and ye rest of the howse had suped) wentt to a play called *hide and seek*, and sometimes hee would hide himselfe so well that in halfe an howers time they could not find him. His Highnese had so used them to this, that when hee wentt really away they thought hee was butt att the usuall sport. A litle before the Duke wentt to super that night hee called for the gardiner, who only had a treble key besides that wch ye Duke had, and bid him give him that key till his owne was mended, wch hee did. And after his Highnese had suped, hee imeadiately called to goe to ye play, and wentt downe the privy staires into the garden, and opened the gate that goes into the parke, treble locking all the doores behind him. And att the garden gate C. B. waited for his Highnese, and putting on a cloake and periwig huried him away to the parke gate, where a coach waited y^t caried them to ye watter side, and, taking the boate that was apointed for that service, they rowed to the staires next the bridge, where I and Miriam waited in a private howse hard by that C. B. had prepared for dresing his Highnese, where all things were in a readinese. Butt I had many feares, for C. B. had desired mee, if they came nott there precisely by ten a' clocke, to shift for my selfe, for then I might conclude they were discovered, and so my stay there could doe noe good, but prejudice my selfe. Yett this did nott make mee leave the howse, though ten a'clock did strike, and hee that was intrusted offten wentt to the landing place and saw noe boate comming was much discouraged, and asked mee what I would doe. I told him I came there with a resolution to serve his High[a], and I was fully determined nott to leave that place till I was outt of hopes of doing what I came there for, and would take my hazard. Hee left mee to goe againe to y[e] watter side, and while I was fortifying myselfe against what might arive to mee, I heard a great noise of many as I thought comming up staires, w[ch] I expected to be soldiers to take mee, but it was a pleasing disapoint-mentt, for y[e] first that came in was y[e] Duke, who with much joy I took in my armes and gave God thankes for his safe arivall. His Highnese called " Quickely quickely dress me ;" and, putting of his cloaths, I dresed him in the wemen's habitt that was prepared, w[ch] fitted his Highnese very well, and was very pretty in itt. Affter hee had eaten something I made ready while I was idle lest his Highnese should bee hungry, and having sentt for a Woodstreet cake (w[ch] I knew hee loved) to take in the barge, with as much hast as could bee his Highnese wentt crose the bridge to y[e] staires where the barge lay, C. B. leading him ; and imediately the boatemen plied the oare so well that they were soone outt of sight, having both wind and tide with y[m]. Butt I afterwards heard the wind changed and was so contrary that C. B. told me hee was terribly afraid they should have beene blowne backe againe. And the Duke said, " Doe any thing with mee rather than lett mee goe backe againe," w[ch] putt C. B. to seeke helpe where itt was only to bee had, and, after hee had most fervently suplicated assistance from God, pre-sently the wind blew faire, and they came safely to there intended landing place. Butt I heard there was some deficulty before they gott to y[e] ship at Graves-End, which had like to have discovered them had nott Collonell Washington's lady assisted them.

Affter the Duke's barge was outt of sight of y[e] bridge, I and Miriam wentt where I apointed the coach to stay for mee, and made drive as fast as y[e] coachman could to my brother's howse, where I staid. I mett none in the way that gave mee any aprehension that the designe was discovered, nor was itt noised abroad till the next day, for (as I related before) ye Duke having used to play at hide and seeke, and to conceale himselfe a long time when they mist him att the same play, thought hee would have discovered himselfe as formerly when they had given over seeking him. Butt a much longer time beeing past than usually was spentt in that deverttissementt, some began to aprehend that his Highnese was gone in earnest past their finding, wch made the Earle of Northumberland (to whose care he was committed) affter strict search made in the howse of S^t. James and all thereabouts to noe purpose, to send and aquaint the Speaker of the House of Commons that the Duke was gone, butt how or by what meanes hee knew nott, butt desired that there might bee orders sentt to the Cinque Ports for stoping all ships going outt till the passengers were examined and search made in all suspected places where his Highnese might be concealed. Though this was gone aboutt with all the vigillancy immaginable, yett itt pleased God to disapointt them of there intention by so infatuating those severall persons who were imployed for writting orders that none of them were able to writt one right, butt ten or twelve of y^m were cast by before one was according to their mind. This accountt I had from Mr. N. who was mace-bearer to the Speeker all that time and a witnese of itt. This disorder of the clarkes contributed much to the Duke's safety, for hee was att sea before any of the orders came to the ports, and so was free from what was designed if they had taken his Highnese.

Though severalls were suspected for being accesory to the escape, yett they could nott charge any with itt butt the person who wentt away, and hee being outt of there reach, they tooke noe notice as either to examine or imprison others. Affter C. B. had beene so successfull in serving the Duke, the Prince imployed him and commanded him backe againe to London, with severall instructions that might have beene serviceable to the King, had nott God Almighty thought fitt to blast all indeavers that might have conduced to his Maties safety. As soone as C. B. landed beyond ye Tower, hee writt

to desire I would doe him the faver as to come to him, as beeing the
only person who att that time hee could trust ; and when hee should
aquaint mee with y⁰ occation of his comming, hee doupted nott
butt I would forgive him for the liberty hee had taken.   I knowing
hee could come upon no accountt but in order to serve the King, I
imediately sent for an honest hackney coachman who I knew might
bee trusted, and taking Miriam with mee, I wentt where hee was,
who giving mee a short information of what hee was employed
aboutt, and how much secresy was to be used both as to yᵉ King's
interest and his owne security, itt is nott to be doupted butt I contributed what I could to both, and, taking him backe in the coach
with mee, left him att a private lodging nott very farre from my
brother's howse, that a servantt of his had prepared for him.   The
earnest desire I had to serve the King made mee omitt noe opertunity wherein I could bee usefull, and the zeale I had for his Matʸ
made me nott see what inconveniencys I exposed myselfe to; for my
intentions being just and inocentt made mee nott reflect what conclusions might bee made for the private visitts which I could nott
butt nesesarily make to him in order to the King's service, for
whatever might relate to itt yᵗ came within my knowledge I gave
him accountt of, and hee made such use of itt as might most advance
his designe.   As long as there was any posibility of conveying
letters secrettly to the King, hee frequently writt, and receaved very
kind letters from his Maᵗⁱᵉ, with severall instructions and letters to
persons of honour and loyalty; butt, when all access was debarred
by the strict guard placed aboutt the King, all hee could then doe was
to keepe warme those affections in such as hee had influence in till
a seasonable opertunity to evidence their love and duty to his Maᵗⁱᵉ.

Though C. B. discovered himselfe to none but such as were
of known integrity, yett many comming to that place where hee lay
made him think itt convenientt for his own safety to goe some time
into the country, and att his returne to bee more private.   One
evening when I wentt to see him I found him lying upon his bed,
and asking him if hee were nott well, hee told mee he was well

enough, butt had receaved a visitt in the morning from a person
that hee wondred much how hee found him out; he was a soli-
cittor that was imployed by all the gentlemen in the county
where hee lived, wch was hard by where his wife dwelt, and he
had brought him word shee was dead, and named the day and
place where shee was buried. I confese I saw him nott in much
griefe, and therefore I used nott many words of consolation,
butt left him affter I had given him accountt of the busynese
I wentt for. I neither made my visitts lese nor more to him
for this news, for Loyalty beeing the principle that first led mee
to a freedome of converse with him, so still I continued itt as
offten as there was occation to serve that interest. Hee putt on
mourning, and told the reason of itt to such as hee conversed with,
butt had desired the gentleman who had first aquainted him with
itt nott to make itt puplicke lest the fortune hee had by his wife
and shee injoyed while shee lived should bee sequestred. To bee
short, affter a litle time hee one day, when I was alone with him,
began to tell mee that now hee was a free man hee would say that
to mee wch I should have never knowne while hee lived if itt had
beene other ways, which was, that hee had a great respect and
honour for mee since the first time hee knew mee, butt had resolved
itt should die with him if hee had not beene in a condittion to
declare itt withoutt doing mee prejudice, for hee hoped if hee
could gaine an interest in my affection itt would nott apeare so
unreasonable to marry him as others might representt itt, for if itt
pleased God to restore the King, of which hee was nott yett outt of
hopes, hee had a promise of beeing one of his Maties bedchamber;
and, though that should faile, yett what hee and I had together
would be about eight hundred pound sterling a yeare, w^ch, with the
Lord's blesing, might be a competency to any contentmentt minds.
Hee so offten insisted on this when I had occation to be with him
that att last hee prevailed with mee, and I did consentt to his pro-
posal, and resolved to marry him as soone as itt apeared convenientt;
butt wee delayed it till wee saw how itt pleased God to determine

of the King's affaires. I know I may bee condemned as one that
was too easily prevailed with, butt this I must desire to bee considered, hee was one who I had beene conversantt with for severall
yeares before; one that professed a great freindship to my beloved
brother Will; hee was unquestionably loyall, handsome, a good
skollar, wch gave him the advantages of writting and speaking well,
and the cheefest ornamentt hee had was a devout life and conversation. Att least hee made itt apeare such to mee, and what ever
misfortune hee brought upon mee I will doe him that right as to
acknowledge I learnt from him many excellent lessons of piety and
vertue, and to abhorre and detest all kinds of vice. This beeing his
constant dialect made mee thinke myselfe as secure from ill in his
company as in a sanctuary. From the prejudice wch that opinion
brought upon mee I shall advise all never to thinke a good intention
can justify what may bee scandalous, for though one's actions bee
never so inocentt, yett they cannott blame them who suspect them
guilty when there is apearance of there deserved reproach; and I
confese I did justly suffer ye scourge of the toung for exposing my
selfe upon any consideration to what might make mee liable to itt,
for which I condemne my selfe as much as my severest enemy.

The King's misfortune dayly increasing, and his enemy's rage
and malice, both were att last determined in that execrable murder,
never to be mentioned without horror and detestation. This putt
such a dampe upon all designes of the Royall party, that they were
for a time like those that dreamed; but they quickly roused up
themselves, and resolved to leave noe meanes unesayed that might
evidence their loyalty. Many excellent designes were laid, butt
the Lord thought fitt to disapoint them all, that His owne power
might bee ye more magnified by bringing home ye King in peace
when all hostile attempts failed. In the meane time C. B. was
nott idle though unsuccessfull, and still continued in or about
London, where hee could bee most secure. One day when I
wentt to see him I found him extreordinary melancholy; and,
having taken mee by the hand, and lead mee to a seate, wentt

from mee to the other side of ye roome, wch I wondred att, because hee usually satte by mee when I was with him. With a deepe sigh hee said, " You must nott wonder att this distance, for I have had news since I saw you, that, if itt bee true, my distance from you must be greater, and I must conclude my selfe the most unfortunate of men." I was much troubled att the discourse, butt itt was increased when hee told mee the reason of itt, for hee said one had informed him that his wife was living. What a surprise that was to mee none can imagine, because I beleeve none ever met with such a tryall. Hee, seeing mee in great disorder, said, " Pray bee not discomposed till the truth bee knowne, for upon the first intimation of itt I sent away my man Ned B., who served mee long and knows the country and persons where she lived, who will returne within a fortnight. It itt be false, I hope you will have no reason to change your thoughts and intentions; if it should bee true, God is my wittnese I am nott guilty of the contrivance of the report of her beeing dead, nor had noe designe butt what I thought justifiable." I could not contradict what hee said, and charity led mee to beleeve him. I left him in great disturbance, butt could conclude nothing till the returne of his servantt, who brought word that his wife died att the same time that hee first gott knowledge of itt, and that hee was att her grave where shee was buried, wch I beleeving, continued my former resolutions, and intended to marry as soone as wee could putt our affaires in such order as to preventt sequestration.

About this time my brother Will came home much discontented, as hee had great reason, for some persons, who mayde itt there busynese to sow the seed of jelousy betwixt the King and Duke of Yorke, in pursuite of that accused my brother that hee kept a corespondence with C. B., who staid att London to hold intelligence in Scotland, and ther designe was to have the Duke of Yorke come there to be crowned King. Though the King did not beleave itt. as hee told my brother when hee sentt for him, yett such was his presentt condittion that hee must either banish him or els disobleige those persons whose service was most useful to him. This his Matie expresed with some trouble; butt, Will, (sayd hee,) to shew you I give noe creditt to this accusation, when ever you heare I am in Scotland (where I hope shortly to bee) come to mee and you shall have no doupt of my kindnesse. My brother humbly intreated his Matie to lett him knowe his accusers and putt him to a tryall, and if they could make good what they charged him with hee would willingly die. "Noe, (says the King,) I will nott tell you who they are, and if you have any suspittion of the persons I charge you upon your allegiance, and as you expect my faver hereafter, nott to challenge them upon itt." Thus with great injustice and sevearity was my brother banished the three courts, the King's, Queene Mother's, and the Princese Royall's. When hee came outt from ye King a gentleman tooke him in his armes who expresed great kindnesse and much trouble for his ill usage, who hee knew undouptedly to bee one of his greatest enemys. All hee said to him was, "You know the King hath tied mee up, and therefore I will say noe more." Had not duty and former obligations beene a tye to all hee was capable to performe, itt was butt an ill requittall for many yeares faithfull service and much hardship, with hazard of his life, for none could brand him with disloyalty or cowardice, nor did hee know how to refuse any imploymentt y^t was serviceable to the King though never so dangerous to undertake.

Butt this injury contributed through the mercy of God to his eternall good, for hee tooke ship imediately, and landed neere Cobham, where, by the faver of the D. and D. of Richmond, hee was well entertained; butt nothing could free him of the great melancholy hee tooke, for, as a person of worth told mee who was a wittnese of itt, hee would steale from the company, and going into the wood and lye many houres together upon the ground, where perhaps he catched cold, and that, mixing with discontented humours, turned to a feaver whereoff hee died. Butt I blese God I had ye sattisfaction to see him dye as a good Christian, for, as soone as hee found himself distempered, hee writt to mee to gett him a private lodging neere the watter side, which I did, and hee comming there imediately wentt to bed, and never rise outt of itt. Affter hee had given mee accountt of what I have now related hee told mee hee had heard Doctor Wild preach att Cobham, and that hee was extreamely well pleased with his sermon, and desired mee to inquire for him, and intreat him to come to him, wch hee did willingly and frequently, and they had both much sattisfaction in one another. My brother beeing desirous to receave the comunion, the Doctor apointed the next morning for ye celebration, butt before wee were to comunicate, my brother said, "I am now going to partake of that most holy sacramentt, and shortely affter to give an accountt to God Almighty for all my actions in this life, and I hope, S^r, (said hee to Doctor W.) you will beleeve I durst nott speake an untruth to you now, and therefore I take this time to assure you that I am nott guilty of what they have accused mee of to the King, and I desire you to vindicate mee." I asked him if hee thought C. B. had any hand in such a designe. Hee said hee thought hee might say as much for him as for himselfe. So, having sometime composed himselfe affter saying this, the usuall prayers of the church beeing ended, my brother, weake as hee was, putt himselfe upon his knees in the bed, and so receaved the blesed sacramentt, and wee that were with him. Hee had before expresed great charity in forgiving his enemys; and, though hee had told mee who (upon good grounds hee had reason to beleeve) they were, yett hee injoyned mee as I loved him to forgive them, for they had proved his best freinds, for, by there meanes, hee came to see the vanity of the world, and to seeke affter the blesednesse of that life wch is unchangeable. While hee lay sicke, C. B. came once to see him, and butt once, because there was search made for him.

The constantt attendance I gave my brother kept mee from seeing C. B. or sending offten to him; but early one morning one of his sarvants came and told mee that, beeing sentt early outt, as they returned they saw an officer with some soldiers marching that way where hee privately lay, and that hee feared his master was betraid.

I then tooke my sister into the next roome and told her I must
now comunicate something to her that I had concealed as knowing
shee would nott aprove of my inttention, butt all considerations
beeing now laid aside I must owne the concerne I had for C. B.,
and wth teares beged of her by all the kindnese shee had for mee,
or if ever shee desired to contribute anything to my contenttment,
that shee would make inquiry what was become of C. B., and
asist him to escape if itt was posible. The trouble shee saw
me in prevailed so with her that itt made her say litle as to
what I might expect of sevearity, and tooke a coach and wentt
imediately where shee thought itt most likely to doe him service,
and itt proving butt a false alarum served only to make him the
more circumspect, and did afterwards something justify mee that I
att that time owned to my sister my resolution of marrying him.

My brother's feaver increasing and his strength decaying, a
few days putt an end to his conflict, for as death was wellcome to
him so hee came peaceably as a freind and nott an enemy, for I
beleeve never any died more composedly of a feaver in the strengh
of there youth. Hee seldome or never raved nor expresed much of
dissatisfaction att the usage hee had mett with; only once hee said,
Were I to live a thousand yeares I would never sett my foott within
a court againe, for there is nothing in itt butt flattery and falshood.

Affter my brother was buried in the Savoy church, neere my
father and mother, within few days I wentt againe to my brother
Murray's, where I staid till the impertunity of my Lady H. prevailed with me to goe home with her to the North. My brother
and sister aproved of itt, and C. B. most willingly consentted to
itt, resolving sodainly to follow mee and puplickly to avow what
wee intended, and to live with a gentleman, a friend of his that was
a great Royallist, where hee expected to be wellcome till such time
as wee found itt convenientt for us to returne where wee had
more interest. This beeing determined, I left all that concerned mee
in such hands as hee advised, with hopes of preventing sequestration,
butt itt fell outt unhapily, as many things els did, and occationed

greater inconvenience. One of the great motives that invited mee
to goe North was that itt began to be discoursed of amongst many
Parliament men that I had beene instrumentall in the Duke's escape,
and, knowing that severall weemen were secured upon lese grounds,
I thought itt best to retire for a time outt of the noise of itt. Itt
was nott withoutt trouble that I left my brother and sister, butt
finding itt nesesary made itt the more easy. Wee began our journy
September 10th, 1649, and had nothing all the way to disturbe us till
wee came to H., beyond Yorke, to a house of Sir C. H., where his
sisters lived. There in one night both Sir C. and his lady fell so
extreamely ill with vomitting and purging in so great violence yt
nothing butt death was expected to them both, and some were so
ill natured as to say they were poisoned, butt itt pleased God they
recovered. And then there son tooke the small poxe, who was
about 3 yeare old, his feaver great and apearance of being extreordinary full; and by the advise of Sr Thomas Gore (who studied
phisicke more for devertisement then gaine) hee tooke a purge
which carried away a great part of yo humour, so that nature, as
hee said, would bee able to master the rest, and itt had so great
succese that hee recovered perfectly well withoutt the least prejudice. I cannott butt mention this from the extreordinarynese of
the cure. As soone as his health would allow of travaile, wee tooke
journy and came to N. Castle, where I was so obleigingly intertained by Sr Ch. and his lady, and with so much respect from the
whole familly, that I could nott butt thinke my selfe very hapy in
so good a societty, for they had an excellent governed familly,
having great affection for one another; all there servantts civill and
orderly; had an excellent preacher for there chaplaine, who preached
twice every Sunday in ye chapell, and dayly prayers morning and
evening. Hee was a man of a good life, good conversation, and
had in such veneration by all as if hee had beene there tutelar
angell. Thus we lived sometime together, with so much peace and
harmony as I thought nothing could have given an interruption to
itt. Butt itt was too great to last long, for the post (going by

weekely) one day brought mee sad letters; one from C. B. giving mee accountt that just the night before hee intended to come North, having prepared all things for accomplishing what we had designed, hee was taken and secured in the Gate-house att Westminster, and could expect nothing butt death. With much dificulty hee had gott that conveyed outt to mee to lett mee know what condittion hee was in, and that hee expected my prayers, since nothing els I could doe could be avealable, for hee had some reason to aprehend those I was concerned in and might have influence upon was his enemys, and therefore I might expect litle assistance from them. Presently affter I receaved a letter from my brother M. and another from my sister N., his very seveare, hers more compasionate, but both representing C. B. under ye caracter of the most unworthy person living; that hee had abused mee in pretending his wife was dead, for shee was alive; and that her unckle Sir Ralph S. had assured them both of itt, wch made nott only them butt all that ever had kindnese for mee so abhorre him, that, though he were now likely to dye, yett none pittyed him. Had the news of either of these come singly itt had beene enough to have tryed the strengh of all the relligion and vertue I had, butt so to bee surrounded with misfortunes conquered what ever could resist them, and I fell so extreamely sicke that none expected life for mee. The care and concerne of S^r Ch. and his lady was very great, who sent post to Newcastle for a phisitian, butt hee beeing sicke could nott come, butt sentt things wch proved ineffectuall. My distemper increased, and I grew so weake I could hardly speake. Aprehending ye aproach of death, I desired my Lady H. to vindicate mee to my brother and sister, for as I was ignorant and inocentt of the guilt they taxed mee with, so I beleeved C. B. was; and therefore I earnestly intreated her to writte to her father to bee his friend, and that malice might nott bee his ruine, wch shee promised; and having taken my last leave (as I thought) of them all, I desired Mr. N. (the chaplaine) to recomende mee to the hands of my Redeemer, and I lay waiting till my change should

come, and all was weeping aboutt mee for that I expected as the
greatest good. Butt itt seemes the mercy of God would nott
then condemne mee into hell, nor his justice suffer mee to goe to
heaven; and therefor continued mee longer upon earth that I might
know the infinitenese of his power who could suport mee under
that load of calamitys. Having laine some houres speechlese (how
I employed that time may hereafter be knowne, if the Lord thinke
fitt to make itt usefull unto any), I began to gape many times one
after another, and I found sencibly like a returne of my spiritts, w^{ch}
Mrs. Cullcheth seeing, came to mee and told mee if I saw another in
that condittion I could prescribe what was fitt for them; and therefore itt were a neglect of duty if I did not use what meanes I
thought might conduce to my recovery. Her discourse made mee
recollect what. I had by mee that was proper for mee. I called
to Crew (who served mee) for itt, and with ye use of some cordialls,
I sencibly grew better, to the sattisfaction of all that was about
mee. I confese death at that time had beene extreamely wellcome; but having intirely resigned myselfe up to the disposall of
my gracious God, I could repine att nothing hee thought fitt to
do with mee, for I knew hee could make either life or death
for my advantage. Though that was great disturbance to mee
wch my brother and sister had written to mee concerning C. B.
wife's being alive, yett I gave nott the least creditt to itt, because I thought there information might come from such as
might report itt out of malice or designe, for none of her relations loved him because hee was nott of there principles. And
a considerable part of her portion being still in there hands, I
judged it might bee still to keep that they raised that story,
which had little influence upon mee, because I gave itt noe
beleefe, only looked upon itt as a just punishmentt to have that
thought true now wch I once mentioned when I thought itt
nott true, only to conceale my intentions; for my Lord H. and
my sister Murray (having observed C. B. come sometimes when
he durst steale abroad to see mee,) said to mee one night, " I

lay a wager you will marry C. B." I smiled and said, " Sure, you would nott have mee marry another woman's husband!" They replied, they knew nott hee had beene maried; upon which I told them whose neece she was (whom they both knew) that was his wife. Butt I did nott say shee was dead, though att that time I beleeved it ; and therefore now looked on this as inflicted for my disimulation, for God requireth truth in the inward parts, and I have a thousand times beged his pardon for that failing.

Upon these grounds itt was that I gave so litle intertainmentt to that story, and all my trouble and feares was affter I began to recover for C. B., lest the Parliamentt should condemne [him] to dye, as they had many gallant gentlemen before ; butt I was much suported one day by reading what fell outt to bee part of my morning devotion (Psa. 102, vers. 19, 20): " For hee hath looked downe from ye height of his sanctuary ; from heaven did the Lord behold the earth. To heare the groaning of the prisoner ; to loose those that are apointed to death." I cannott omitt to mention this because itt was so seasonable a promise, and I was so asisted by faith to rely upon itt that in a manner itt overcame all my feares. To confirme itt is nott in vaine to beleeve and expect promised mercys, within few days there came severall letters both to Sir C. H., his lady, and my selfe, yt C. B. had made his escape outt of the Gate-house just the night before hee was to have beene brought to his tryall. None then could give accountt how or by what meanes hee had gott outt, butt afterwards I was informed by the person hee employed, that having with much dexterity conveyed into him a glase of aqua fortis, hee, with that and much paines, cutt the iron bars of ye window asunder, butt lett itt stand by a litle hold till the time was fitt to make use of itt, and then, having found meanes to appointt such as hee relyed upon to bee under the window at such a time as the guards were past that tour, hee tooke ye ropes of the bed and fastened them to some part of the window, and so wentt downe by them, butt his weight made them faile, and hee fell downe nott without hurt, butt the next

dificulty was a pailing that was aboutt the verge of the window,
butt his asistants by standing upon one another's shoulders, reached
over to him and gott him over the pailing, and so escaped the fury
of his enemys; wch many was glad of, and more had joyned with
them if they had nott beene posesed with a prejudice against him
for the injury they suposed hee had done mee in persuading mee
his wife was dead when shee was alive. Butt hee nott being now
in a capacity to vindicate himselfe, itt was easy to lay upon him
what guilt they pleased ; butt all that his enemys could alleadge
never prevailed with mee to lessen one graine of my concerne for
him, because all they could say was the report y^t shee was living,
butt they never named the person that could testify itt from there
owne knowledge, except such as might bee biased by what I have
mentioned allready. I cannott butt acknowledge I had great sattisfaction in the news of his escape, and, though I was sometimes disturbed because I heard nott from him where hee was or how, yett I
pleased myselfe with ye hopes hee was well and secure, and so y^e
better dispensed with my wantt of letters, since I knew he could
nott convey them withoutt hazard of being discovered.

Itt is nott to bee imagined by any pious vertuous person (whose
charity leads them to judge of others by themselves,) butt that I
looked upon itt as an unparaleld misfortune, how inocentt so ever
I was, to have such an odium cast upon mee as that I designed to
marry a man that had a wife, and I am sure none could detest mee
so much as I abhored the thought of such a crime. I confese I
looked upon itt as the greatest of afflictions; butt, that I might nott
sett limitts to myself, the Lord thought fitt to shew hee could make
mee suffer greater and yett suport mee under them. The first
Sunday that my health and strengh would permitt mee to goe outt
of my chamber, I went to the chapell in the morning (with ye rest
of ye familly) to offer up thanksgiving to my God who had raised
mee from ye gates of death ; and affter dinner retiring into my
chamber, as I usually did, the door beeing locked and I alone, I
was reading a sermon with wch I was very well pleased, butt on a

sodaine I was so disordered and in so great an agony that I
thought itt nott fitt to be alone, and all the servantts beeing at
dinner, and none within my call, I wentt imediately to M^r N.
chamber, who was much surprised seeing mee come in so much
disordered. I freely told him every circumstance, imagining hee
was a person fitt to intrust with any disorder of my soule, and
desired his prayers; which the Lord blest with so good successe, y^t I
imediately left trembling, and found a great serenity both of mind
and body. Having giving him thanks for the great concerne hee
shewed for mee, and had his promise to conceale what I had comunicated to him, I left him to goe and make myselfe ready for
attending my Lady H. to the chapell, thinking myselfe as secure of
what I had said to him as if itt had beene within my owne breast,
where itt should have beene still if I had then beene aquainted, as
I have beene offten since, with the effects of melancholy vapours,
butt having never known them before in others or my selfe made
them apeare the more dreadfull; but those who have experience of
them will I hope have the more charity for mee when they consider
what effects they have had upon themselves.

I am sory I cannott relate my owne misfortunes withoutt reflecting
upon those who was the occation of them, especially beeing one of
y^t profession that I have ever looked upon with great respect. I
have allready given a caracter of Mr. N. parts and practise, and how
much he was valued by all the familly and such as conversed with
him. One day hee having preached at Carlile at the meeting for
the sise, when hee came home hee came to my chamber and told
mee hee had left Sr Charles, and came home with Mr Cule., who
had entertained him by the way with many variety of discourse,
butt amongst the rest (said hee,) hee tells mee that my Lady H.
is jelouse of S^r Ch. and you. I was strangely surprised to heare
that, and said sure he was drunk, for, as I am sure I never gave her
the least occation, I am confidentt shee knows her owne interest
so great in S^r Ch. that shee need not feare beeing suplanted by
any; and besides, she knows all the concerne I can have for any

re her were there nothing els;
ng the least thought that shee
I had itt," said hee, " from any
butt noe doupt hee hath had itt
overnese to her before shee was
l her concernes." Hee insisted
any argumentts to confirme hee
withall that hee had observéd
icc as formerly, and that hee
icc should use one so ill who
come to a remote place outt
I found nothing of alteration
:ell her what I heard (though
the long friendship betwixt us
hee were guilty of the imper-
ght dispose of mee how shee
:faction. " Can you imagine
·u shee is jelouse? Noe; shee
'hat will you then advise mee
shee is of so odd a humour,
a case what to advise.   I
upon as one of the finest
gentlemen in the nation ; and had hee had ye good fortune to
have had you to have beene his wife, hee had been the hapiest
man alive." All I concluded att that time was, that hee should
bee free in telling mee what ever hee saw in my cariage that
looked like giving ground for such a suspittion. With many
serious protestations hee freed mee for giving any occation, butt
dayly gave mee accountt of ye increase of itt.   To bee as
short as the circumstances will allow, hee was never with mee
butt hee magnified S^r Ch. up to the skys; spoke much to
his lady's disadvantage ; butt what hee said of mee was so
greatly allied to flattery that I should have obhored itt from
any other that had nott apeared as hee did. At last I began

sodaine I was so disordered an
thought itt nott fitt to be alon
dinner, and none within my ca
chamber, who was much surpris
disordered. I freely told him ev
was a person fitt to intrust wit
desired his prayers; which the Lo
imediately left trembling, and fo
and body. Having giving him
shewed for mee, and had his pror
nicated to him, I left him to
attending my Lady H. to the ch
what I had said to him as if itt
where itt should have beene stil
I have beene offten since, with
butt having never known them
them apeare the more dreadfull
them will I hope have the more
what effects they have had upon

I am sory I cannott relate my
upon those who was the occatio
y^t profession that I have ever

have allready given a caracter of Mr. N. parts and practise, and how
much he was valued by all the familly and such as conversed with
him. One day hee having preached at Carlile at the meeting for
the sise, when hee came home hee came to my chamber and told
mee hee had left Sr Charles, and came home with Mr Cule., who
had entertained him by the way with many variety of discourse,
butt amongst the rest (said hee,) hee tells mee that my Lady H.
is jelouse of S^r Ch. and you. I was strangely surprised to heare
that, and said sure he was drunk, for, as I am sure I never gave her
the least occation, I am confidentt shee knows her owne interest
so great in S^r Ch. that shee need not feare beeing suplanted by
any; and besides, she knows all the concerne I can have for any

is already fixed, and that may secure her were there nothing els;
butt I am very farre from intertaining the least thought that shee
can have any such suspittion. " If I had itt," said hee, " from any
other hand, I would thinke so too; butt noe doupt hee hath had itt
from his wife, who you know was governese to her before shee was
maried, and is still intrusted with all her concernes." Hee insisted
much on this discourse, and used many argumentts to confirme hee
had reason to beleeve itt true, and withall that hee had observed
of late shee was not so kind to mee as formerly, and that hee
thought itt a strange thing that shee should use one so ill who
had left all relations and friends to come to a remote place outt
of kindness to her. I assured him I found nothing of alteration
in her, and that I was resolved to tell her what I heard (though
nott the author), and expected from the long friendship betwixt us
that ingenuity as freely to owne if shee were guilty of the imperfection of jelousy, and that shee might dispose of mee how shee
pleased, in order to her owne sattisfaction. " Can you imagine
(said hee,) that shee will owne to you shee is jelouse? Noe; shee
hath too much pride for that." " What will you then advise mee
to doe?" I replied. " The truth is, shee is of so odd a humour,
(said hee,) that it is hard in such a case what to advise. I
hartily pitty Sr Ch., who I look upon as one of the finest
gentlemen in the nation ; and had hee had ye good fortune to
have had you to have beene his wife, hee had been the hapiest
man alive." All I concluded att that time was, that hee should
bee free in telling mee what ever hee saw in my cariage that
looked like giving ground for such a suspittion. With many
serious protestations hee freed mee for giving any occation, butt
dayly gave mee accountt of ye increase of itt. To bee as
short as the circumstances will allow, hee was never with mee
butt hee magnified Sr Ch. up to the skys; spoke much to
his lady's disadvantage ; butt what hee said of mee was so
greatly allied to flattery that I should have obhored itt from
any other that had nott apeared as hee did. At last I began

to observe my Lady H. grow more reserved than usuall, and the whole familly abate much of there respect; only S^{r} Ch. continued as formerly to mee. I used dayly to be till five a' clock with my Lady H. working, or any other devertisement that shee imployed her selfe in, and then retired to my chamber for halfe an hower; then Sr Charles and his lady came and staid with mee (till the time wee wentt to ye chapell), either playing on the gitarre or with ye chilldren that lay neere me, or discoursing, and this was for a long time our constant practice. Butt on a sodaine I found an allteration, for my Lady H. would come to the doore with Sir C., butt when hee came in shee wentt into the chilldren's chamber, which I observing followed her and left Sir C. in my chamber. One night as I was thus going outt to follow his lady he pulled mee backe and would nott lett mee goe, and ye more presing hee was to have me stay the more earnest I was to goe, butt seeing hee was resolute I staid. Hee told mee hee had observed of late that I was growne very strange to him, and that when ever hee came in I wentt outt of my chamber. I said itt was only to waite upon his lady, and therfore hee could nott take itt ill. Hee saw mee in great disorder, and was very urgentt to know what the reason of itt was. I confese the teares were in my eyes, which hee seeing vowed hee would nott goe outt of the roome till I resolved him. I told him I would upon the condition hee would promise nott to speake of itt to any person, and that hee would doe what I should desire. Hee said hee would if it were in his power, and bid mee bee free with him. I said, "Sir C. I confese I have receaved much civility from you ever since I came into your familly, and as I know you shewed itt as a testimony of your affection to your lady because I had an interest in her faver, so I valued itt upon y^{t} accountt, and nott as I beleeved I deserved itt; but now I must desire you as you respect your selfe, as you love your lady, or have any regard to mee, retrench your civility in to more narrow bounds, els you may prejudice your selfe in the opinion of those who thinke mee unworthy your converse." Hee grewe angry, and said hee must know who those

persons were ; I said hee must pardon mee, for that itt was enough
I had told him how hee might preventt an inconvenience, and if
hee either devulged what I had said, or did nott performe the
condittion in doing what I desired, I would goe outt of his howse
upon the first discovery. I left him affter I said this and wentt to
his lady, who sometimes would be free enough, another time so
reserved as shee would hardly speake to mee, either at table or any
other time, which made mee then give the more creditt to what
Mr. N. had told mee of her; butt againe I was att a stand when
being alone with her one day shee told mee she knew nott what to
thinke of Mr. N., but shee bid mee bee upon my guard when I
conversed wth him, for shee assured mee hee was not my friend
so much as I beleeved. I thanked her for her advise, butt knew
nott what to conclude, because hee had posesed mee with an
opinion that she was lesened in her respect to him because hee
was so civill to mee; but this I concealed from her, knowing itt was
upon another ground, wch may nott bee amisse to insert here.

There was two young ladys in the howse who had beene bred up
Papists, and by Sir Ch: example and care was turned Protestants.
These two Sr C. recomended to Mr. N.'s care to instruct them in the
principles of our relligion, and they dayly wentt to his chamber,
sometimes together, sometimes alone, as there conveniency led
them. They beeing very young, and hugely vertuous and inocentt,
and having Sir C. order for going frequently to his chamber,
thought the offtener they wentt the better, and sometimes affter
super would goe and stay there an hower or two. They had a
discreet woman attended them, who I had recomended. Shee
came to mee one morning and told mee shee could nott butt
aquaint mee with something that shee would seek my advise in;
I said I would give itt freely. Says shee, " You know I am intrusted with the care of these young ladys, and that S^r Ch. orders
them to goe frequently to Mr. N. chamber; butt I have observed
the eldest of them stay much longer then the other, and to goe
affter super, and sometimes stay there till 12 a' clocke, and

though I have gone severall times to call her, yett she would nott
come with me." I said I was sory to hear that ; for, though I did
beleeve shee might as inocently converse with him as with her
brother, yett itt might give occation of reflection upon them both,
wch I wished might bee prevented, butt withoutt saying anything
to S^r Ch. or his lady. This fell outt to bee aboutt the beginning of
my Lady H. growing a litle reserved to mee; butt when ever I had
any opertunity of conversing with her I still brought in some discourse of love and friendship and jelousy, and that sometimes itt
might bee where there was greatest intimacy; butt if I could have a
suspition of any person that I thought worth my friendship, shee
would bee the first person her selfe that I would declare itt to, for if
shee were vertuous there is nothing I could desire her to doe that
shee would omitt for my sattisfaction, and if I beleeved her vicious
she were nott worthy my converse. I uttered this with more than
an ordinary sence, wch I thought made some impresion of her; and
I thought I was fully confirmed, when early one morning shee came
into my chamber before I was outt of my bed, and lying downe by
me shee said, " I have so much confidence of your friendship and
discretion, that I am come to secke your advise and assistance how
to manage what I have of late discovered, that if nott prevented
will make great disorder amongst us." I tooke her in my armes
with great joy, and told her shee might as freely comunicate anything to mee as to her owne hart, for I should bee fast in conccaling
and active in doing what ever shee pleased to intrust mee with;
beeing fully perswaded if shee were guilty of that imperfection of
jelousy shee was now come to aquaint mee with itt, and to advise
aboutt a remedy. Butt I was in a mistake; for shee told mee shee
had of late made some litle observation that Mrs F., who was the
eldest of the two sisters, was looked upon more kindly by M^r N.
then was usuall with his gravity; wch gave her the curiosity the day
before, when she wentt out of the dining-roome affter dinner, all
the company being gone, and remembring shee had left them two
together, shee turned backe, and looking through the crany of the

doore shee saw Mr. N. pull her to him, and with much kindnese lay
her head in his bosome.   I said that might bee very inocently done,
though I confesed itt had beene better undone; "for sure hee can
have no ill design, being, I beleeve, a very good man, and she is too
much a child to think of marying her though there were nothing
els to object." Shee said shee was nott so much a child as her stature
made her apeare, and therfore had great aprehensions that yᵉ respect
Sʳ Charles had for him might incourage him to hope, if hee could
gaine her consentt, to obtaine his; "butt if hee should have the least
ground to suspect what I fear, hee would never suffer him in his
sight; and if wee wanted him, you know (says my Lady,) that in these
times we should find itt deficult to gett one in his place who could
so well discharge his duty to our sattisfaction, and yett so discreet as
not to give offence to those of a contrary judgementt, such as most
are hereaboutt." I acknowledged itt was true that her La. said,
and in my opinion itt would bee best for mee to speake (since her
La. would intrust none els with itt,) to him aboutt itt. And I
thought hee was so ingenious a person, and had often profesed to
have so great an opinion of mee, that I thought hee would not conceale his intention from mee, and I should freely give her La. an
accountt of his answeare. I made use of this opertunity to insist
much upon the sattisfaction I had in her long continued friendship,
and that I hoped, what ever my present misfortune was, yett that
shee would make noe conclusions to my prejudice without giving mee
leave to vindicate my selfe ; wᶜʰ shee promised, and left mee, having
ingaged mee to lett none know what had pased betwixt us.

   The first conveniency I had I told Mr. N. that I was going to aske
him a question, and that I desired and expected hee would bee ingenious
in resolving mee, because itt was nott to sattisfy my owne curiosity
butt outt of an intent to serve him, wᶜʰ I could nott doe if hee were
reserved in his answeare. Hee seemed to bee surprised with this
discourse, butt assured mee hee would bee very ingenious. I asked
him then if hee had any inclination for Mrs. F. or any designe to
marry her ; he protested with much seriousnese he had nott.   I

said I was very glad to hear itt, for now with the more confidence I could suprese the suspittion wch some had of itt. " Butt (said hee,) what would you have done if I had confesed I had loved her ?" " Truly (I replied,) I would have representted to you the prejudice you would have brought upon yourselfe; for undouptedly S^r Ch., who is now your great freind, would turne your proffesed enemy, and make all others so that hee had influence upon." Therfore, as his intentions was free from such a designe, so I desired his converse might bee suitable, and I would then indeaver to convince them of there error who apprehended what I had told him.

I gave my Lady H. an accountt of what discourse Mr. N. and I had, wch shee was sattisfied with; butt this was the ground upon wch I knew my Lady H. had nott so good an opinion of Mr. N. as formerly, and therfore I could nott well know what to thinke when my Lady told mee, as I have allready mentioned, that hee was nott my freind so much as I beleaved, nor so good a secretary. I had the same information from her woman to (a discreet person who till that time loved mee well). I thought I would take a triall of him, and the first time hee came into my chamber, hee falling upon his usuall discourse, regretting to see my Lady H. so unkind to mee, I said I confesed I could nott butt look upon itt as my greatest misfortune, and such as swallowed up my former trouble, because to any one that should beleeve mee guilty of such unworthynese as occatioued her unkindnese itt could nott butt bee a confirmation of ye crime laid to my charge with C. B., and the more unpardonable because ignorance in this could bee noe excuse. I said I would comunicate a secrett to him if hee would solemely promise nott to discover itt to any person living; wch hee engaged with all the protestations y^t was fitt for one of his profesion. I told him I was maried, and if hee beleeved I understood what either love or duty tied mee to, that was enough to secure my Lady H. from her aprehensions, though I had never had a value for her friendship. (I confese I only told him this outt of designe to try if hee would speake of itt againe, and was indifferent whether itt was beleeved true or false, since I hoped a litle time would make the discovery.) Hee seemed to be highly sencible of the injury shee did mee, and att my request undertooke to tell her that hee had observed her unkindnese, and as much as was fitt for him to prese for the reason of itt, wch if shee gave, then to asert my inocence and ye wrong shee did bothe to her husband and her selfe ; and in this I thought hee would obleige both them as well as mee. This hee promised, butt how hee performed itt shall bee affter manifest.

I saw dayly my Lady II. grow now to that height of strangenese that when I spoke to her shee would give mee noe answeare, or if shee did, itt was with that slightnese that I could nott butt bee very sencible of itt. And that wch angred mee most was, that when ever S^r Ch. came where I was, hee was ten times more free in his converse then hee had beene before I had spoken to him. These two extreames with my owne presentt condittion was deplorable, having spentt all the mony I brought with mee, beeing in a strange place where I had neither friendship nor aquaintance with any. To London I durstt not goe, for feare of beeing secured upon the accountt of the Duke's escape; and besides, I knew I need not expect any thing butt unkindnese from my brother and sister; and how to send to C. B. to advise with him I knew nott. To stay where I was I had no manner of sattisfaction. And if I had known whither to goe, to leave that familly with such an odium as was laid upon mee, could nott butt make mee unwellcome any where. Thus, when I reflected upon my disconsolate condittion, I could find content in nothing butt in resorting to The hearer of prayer, who never leaves or forsakes those who trust in him. To the God of mercy I poured forth my complaint in the bitternese of my soule, and with abundant teares presented my suplication to him that judgeth righteously and did know my inocence, and therefore I interceded for the merits of my Redeemer that hee would deliver mee outt of the trouble that incompased mee round, and direct mee how to dispose of myselfe in y^t sad exegentt that I was in; and having resigned my selfe wholy to the disposall of his will, I did with confidence expect a deliverance, because I knew him whom I trusted.

By the way I cannot omitt to mention what was remarkeable the time I was in that familly. One night, beeing fast asleepe, I was sodainely wakened with the shaking of the bed somewhat violentt, butt of short continuance. In the morning I told Sʳ Ch. and my Lady that I had heard of earthquakes, butt I was confidentt I had felt one that night, and related how itt was. They laughed att mee, and said I had only dreamt of itt. I could nott convince them, nor they mee; butt a litle before dinner came in some gentlemen that lived within 3 or 4 mile, and Sʳ Charles asked them what news: they replied the greatest they knew was that there had beene an earthquake that night, and that severall howses were shaken downe with itt. Then they beleeved what I had told them. Another day my Lady H. and I was sitting together alone in my chamber, aboutt an ell or more distant from on-another, and sodainely the roome did shake, so that both our heads knockt together. Shee looked pale like death, and I beleeve I did the same, and wee were hardly well recovered from our feares when Sʳ C. came in to see how wee were, and told us hee was walking in the gallery with Mr. N. and that they were so shaken they could skarce hold there feett, and was forced to hold themselves on the sides of the howse. These both hapened in the yeare 1649.

Butt to returne where I left. My Lady H. strangenese did nott make mee neglect anything that I usually did before, and one Sunday morning I wentt to her chamber to waite upon her as formerly when shee wentt to the chapell. I found the doore shutt, butt heard her talke to her weemen; so I knockt. One of them came to the doore, and asked who was there. When they knew itt was I, they said they could nott open the doore for there lady was busy. I thought this was a great allteration; however, I said nothing, butt wentt up to walke in the gallery, wᶜʰ was yᵉ usuall passage to the chapell, till shee was ready to goe. I had nott walked a turne or two butt Sʳ Ch. came to mee. I was in disorder, wᶜʰ hee seeing

asked what ailed mee. I told him I found hee had been unjust to mee, and I should bee so just to my selfe in keeping my
promise as that I resolved the next day to leave his howse, for I
could nott suffer to live in any place where I had nott the faver of
the owners. "I know (says hee,) that you take itt ill to see my
wife so strange to you; and shee doth itt a' purpose that you may
inquire the reason of itt from her selfe, and then shee will resolve
you." I said that should nott bee long in doing, nor had itt beene
so long undone, butt that shee had avoided all occations that might
give mee opertunity of speaking to her. (Another reason wch I did
nott mention was that Mr. N. had used many argumentts to diswade
mee from taking notice of itt to her, some of them nott much to her
advantage.)

Wee wentt all to the chapell together, and affter sermon the post
came with letters while wee were att dinner, some to them and
some to mee. I made use of this when wee rose from the table to
tell my Lady H. that I had receaved letters from London, and that
there was something of concerne I had to say to her La^p, and asked
where I might have her alone. Shee told mee shee would come
within a litle while to my chamber; where I wentt, and within a
litle while shee came there, and I taking her in my armes kist her,
and wellcomed her to my chamber as a great stranger. So locking
ye doore wee sate downe. "Madam, (said I,) though I made a letter
the pretence for seeking this faver to speake with you, yett there is
nothing in that worth your La. knowledge, and the only thing I
have to say is to beg of you by all the friendship and kindnese you
ever had for mee to bee free with mee, and lett mee know what I
have done to make you of late so unkind." "Truly (said shee,) I
wondred you were so long inquiring, and resolved till you asked the
question I would never tell you; butt now you have begun lett
mee aske you how you could have the vanity to beleeve S^r Ch. was
in love with you, and I was jealous of you; and have the confidence
to speake of itt to Mr. N. and speake so unworthily of mee as you
have done to him this long time, as if I were the most contemptable

creature living, and that you pittied S^r Ch. for having such a wife ?
Was this done like a freind? Oh! (said shee,) if I had nott had itt
from Mr. N. who is so good a man that I cannott butt beleeve him,
I should never have given faith to itt from any other person." I was
I confese astonished to heare him given as the athour of that accusation, beeing all his owne words wch hee had offten used to mee as his
opinion, butt itt seemes hee had represented them as mine. "Madam,
(said I,) I cannot wonder att y^r strangenese if you beleeved this true,
butt rather how you could suffer such a one within your familly."
"Had I followed Mr. Nicolls advise (shee replied,) I had sentt you
away long since; for hee prest itt offten, and when he could nott
prevaile with mee hee writt to my father, from whom I receaved
a very seveare letter for letting you stay so long with mee. This
I now tell you plainely, to confirme what I once told you before,
that Mr. Nicolls was nott your freind so much as you beleeved,
nor I so unworthy as ye caracter you gave of mee." "Madam, (said
I,) I must acknowledge I did beleeve him my freind, and so excellent a man that I thought, as all in your familly did, that itt was a
blesing to have him in ye howse. Butt now so much the greater is
my misfortune to have him for my accuser, who is so much respected
by all, and whose very profesion would inforce beleefe. I love
nott retaliation, and to returne ill for ill, butt since I have no other
way to asert my owne inocency I must freely declare hee was himselfe the only person that tooke paines to perswade mee you were
jelouse of mee; and when I resolved to vindicate my selfe from
whatever might seeme to give occation for itt, hee diswaded mee,
and said you had too much pride to owne itt, and that you would
butt laugh att mee, and 'twould expose mee to your scorne; and
what hee related as my words were his owne, wch when at any time
I contredicted, hee would say itt was my partiality made mee
defend you, and nott my reason. This, madam, is so great a truth
that I will owne itt before him whenever you find itt convenientt.
But pray, madam, (said I,) when hee told you all these things to my
disadvantage, did itt nott lesen your beleefe of itt comming from a

person who proffesed to have so great respect for mee, and yett per-
forming acts so contrary to itt? Did nott this plead for mee in
your thoughts, that hee who could disemble might bee unjust, and
I inocentt?" "I confese (said my Lady,) itt did prevaile much on
your side, and one day when hee was railing against you I said to
him, How comes you are so civill to her, and profese so great a
esteeme of her, if you have so ill an opinion of her? I an esteeme
of her? (replied hee,) I could nott butt bee civill to her because I
saw S^r Ch. and your La. respect her; butt God is my wittnese I
never looked upon her butt as one of the ayreiest things that ever
I saw, and admired what itt was your La. and S^r Ch. saw in her
to bee so kind to her." I smiled and said, "I wish I could as
easily confirme hee was the author of what hee related of mee, as
I can, under his owne hand, that hee had better thoughts of mee then
so ayry a thing as hee then represented mee." Shee was desirous
to see ye letter; wch I shewed her, with the copy of my owne to w^{ch}
his was an answeare, and was the first letter that ever I copied of
my owne, and fell outt well that I had itt, els his would nott have
been well understood (the occation of itt was, att the first notice I
had of C. B. wife's beeing alive, before itt came to bee publickly
knowne, itt is nott to bee imagined butt itt putt mee in great disorder, and, having none I would communicate itt to, I writt a serious
letter to him representing something of [the] disorder I was in, and
earnestly desired his prayers, to wch his letter answered; and were
itt nott too tedious I should insert them both here). As soon as my
Lady H. read the letter, shee said, "I am afraid this man hath
deceaved us all, and will prove a villaine." While wee were at this
discourse S^r Ch. knoct att the doore; wee lett him in, and he
smiling said, "I hope you understand one another." Wee gave
him some short accountt of what had beene betwixt us, wch hee said
did confirme what hee had beene of opinion of a pritty while;
"butt (sayed hee,) I will injoyne you both, what ever paseth betwixt
you when you are alone, lett noe person know butt that you are
still att the same distance you were before, till my returne; for I am

imediately informed of some mose-troopers that are plundering in
the country, and I and all my men are going to try if wee can take
them ; therfore you must pray for mee, since I cannot goe with you
now to the chapell." Wee both promised to follow his injunctions,
and parted. Though I did what I could to conceale anything of
sattisfaction, yett the joy I had to see some glimps of light apeere
for my vindication putt a visible change upon mee. And my Lady
H. found itt deficult to restraine her former kindnese from apearing
affter shee began to find shee had beene injured as well as I. When
Sr Ch. returned hee was a wittnese of many debates betwixt us.
When shee considered what a person Mr. N. was, shee then condemned mee guilty of all hee accused mee of; but when I urged ye
many yeares experience shee had had of my converse, and whether
shee had ever knowne mee doe any unworthy act, then, when shee
reflected upon that, shee condemned him. Butt, to bee short, shee
concluded that itt was fitt to have her cleared from the aspersion of
jelousy and ye consequences of itt, wch one of us had taxed her with,
and none had more reason to prese that then I who suffred most
by itt. Att last we resolved as the fairest way, for mee to goe to
Mr. N. and tell him that I was resolved to vindicate my selfe, and
therefore to desire him nott to take itt ill if I brought him for a
wittnese of my inocency, who was the first and only person that told
mee of my lady's beeing jelouse, and who had offten assured mee
hee saw nothing in my cariage that could give ye least ground
for itt. Sr C. had left us to our contriveance. And when wee
were determined I left my Lady H., and, apointing the garden
to bee our meeting place, where I was to bring Mr N., I wentt
to his chamber, butt found him nott there. I imediately wentt
alone to the garden, to the walke where my Lady H. and I
had designed to meett, and in the way to itt I saw Sir C.
and Mr. N. very serious together in a close walke. I tooke noe
notice I saw them, butt wentt on to the place apointed; and while
I was walking there I began to consider that itt fell outt well I had
nott mett with Mr. N. alone, for hee that had already injured mee so

much might possibly alleadge that I had prevailed with him to take that upon him hee had never saied only to conceale my guilt, and soe I might still bee thought what hee first represented mee. Therfore I resolved to propose itt to my Lady H. when shee came, to goe together where S^r Ch. and hee was walking, and there speake of itt to him before them. Shee aproved of my reason and resolution, and said itt was very likely hee might make such a use of itt. And that this way would bee more sattisfaction to her then ye other. So wee wentt together to ye close walke where S^r Ch. and hee was walking together. (By the disorder I saw him in, I knew S^r Ch. had given him some hint of what was amongst us, and ye reason hee gave his Lady and I afterwards was, because hee had nott a mind to have him too much surprised, and knew y^t that meeting would nott bee for his advantage.) "Mr. N. (said I,) you could nott butt have observed a great strangenese from my Lady H. to mee a good while, and beeing noe longer able to suffer itt I have presed to know ye reason; and beeing informed of itt, I know itt is in your power to make the reconciliation, and therefore I expect itt from you." "Truly, Mrs. M. (replied hee,) I shall bee very glad to bee an instrumentt in so good a worke." "Then (said I,) Mr. N. doe you nott remember that day you came from Carlile you told mee of a person that informed you my lady was jealous of mee?" "Noe indeed, (said hee,) I remember noe such thing." "Itt is imposible (I replied,) your memory can be so ill; butt to make itt better I will beg leave of S^r Ch. and my lady to whispers the person in your care that you named, because I desire nott to disobleige him with this contest." They both gave leave, and I whispered softly, "Did nott you tell mee Mr. C. told you, and you were shure hee had itt from his wife, and so you could nott doupt the truth of itt?" "I remember indeed (said hee,) that I told you your cariage was such that if you did nott mind itt you would give my lady occation to bee jelouse." I lifted up my eyes and hands to heaven, and said, "Good God! hath this man the confidence to say this?" I turned to S^r Ch. and my lady, and then repeated severall things allready

mentioned, wherein hee had condemned my Lady and magnified
mee to a high degree of flattery. And I said, " I confese itt is a
great disadvantage I have to contest with such a person whom there
is much more reason should bee beleeved then I; but S^r you are a
Justice of Peace, and therfore may lawfully take my oath, and I
will most solemnly give itt upon the Bible that hee did say these
things to mee, and insisted offten on them, and diswaded mee
offten when I was resolved to have justified my selfe to your lady."
" And I (replied hee,) will take my oath upon the same Bible that
itt is nott true shee says." My admiration was such to heare him
speake att y^t rate, that I was allmost strucke dumbe, and all I said
more was very calmely, " Mr. N. you have made more use of y^e
Bible than I have done, and therfore perhaps thinke you may bee
bolder with itt; butt I would nott sweare your oath to have S^r C.
estate." Hee would have insisted; butt S^r Ch. and his lady interupted him, and desired there might bee noe more of itt. I said I
could say noe more then what I had offred, and I left my part to
bee made evidentt by the great and holy God who knew how I was
wronged, and to him I did referre myselfe, who I knew would doe
mee right. My Lady and I then wentt in, and S^r Ch. followed us.
And when wee were together, every one freely gave accountt what
caracter hee had given of us. My Lady and I hee had most equally
balanced together; for whatever ill he had said of mee to her hee
had said as much of her La^s to mee. And as hee indeavored to
poses mee with the opinion of her beeing jelouse, so hee perswaded
her that shee had reason for itt by my beeing desperately in love
with S^r Ch. S^r Ch. laughed att this discourse, and said, " Hee hath
beene so wise as nott to have much of this to mee; only once hee
said that hee was sure you were in love with mee, and I could nott
butt perceave itt; and I told him as I was an honest man I had
never seene anything like itt." " Well, (said I,) then itt seemes in
this hee had something of justice y^t hee had a mind I should thinke
as well of you in gratitude as hee would have your thoughts beene
of mee, for hee gave you high comendations, and one of your ex-

cellentt qualitys was that you had a great value for mee, wch I did then and shall still acknowledge I have receaved much more civilitys from you then I deserved, yet noe more then I might expect from any civill person in there owne howse who loved there lady, and for her sake would obleige those shee loved. Itt was, S^r, (continued I,) upon this accountt that I both receaved and returned what you gave and I paid. And now, before your lady, I conjure you by all the hopes you have of hapinese here or hereafter, and as you would avoid all the curses threatned to disemblers, freely declare what I have ever done or said since I came within your familly that might confirme you of Mr. N. opinion of mee." Hee most solemely declared hee never saw noe ground for itt, and that that was the first thing wch made him aprehend Mr. N. nott beeing what hee should bee by the contrediction hee saw in that. There was nothing more contributed to vindicate mee then the disorder wch from that day apeared in Mr. N.; for itt was visible to the meanest in the howse, though few knew the reason of itt, because S^r Ch. had a respect for him, and desired all should respect him, and therfore did as much as could bee to conceale what had beene amongst us.

Some time affter this the Sacramentt was to bee celebrated in the chapell, and I had many debates with my selfe what to doe. Att last, beeing resolved, I sentt for Mr. N. to my chamber, and told him itt was not withoutt great disputes in my thoughts of the good and ill of partaking or leaving that holy mistery that had made mee send for him ; and though hee had injured mee beyond a posibility of beeing forgiven by any as a woman, yett as a christian I forgave him; and though hee had wronged mee, yett I would nott wrong my selfe by wanting y^t benefit which I hoped for and did expect in that blesed participation. " This (said I,) I thought fitt to tell you that you may nott thinke I goe for coustume or formality, butt with a sence of both my duty and advantage, and lett nott my charity make you thinke litle of y^r fault, for withoutt great repentance great will be your judgement." Hee aproved much of my charity, and would have said something to vindicate himself; butt I

interupted him, and desired him to consider what hee was goeing
aboutt, and that itt would agravate his guilt to thinke to justify
himselfe, since noe excuse could bee made.   I instanced that particular that was an undenyable fault, wch was his going imediately
from mee to tell my Lady Howard that I had as a secrett told him
I was maried. "How can I butt suspect (said I,) the truth of all you
speake outt of the pulpitt, when you devulged that affter such
solemne engagementts of secresy which I only said for a triall of
your fidelity."   "O! (replyed hee,) if you knew what temptation I
had to make that discovery, you would forgive mee."   "Itt was only
to tell you that (said I,) that I sentt for you, and againe I repeat itt
that I doe forgive you, and pray God to make you penitentt for
your sin, that so you may obtaine mercy, and that y^r taking the holy
sacramentt may nott bee for your greater condemnation. And this
is all I have to say to you."   So hee left me.

Affter the solemne time of our devotion was over, I began seriously
to think what way to dispose of myself; for, though S^r Ch. and his
lady were returned to there former kindness, yett I thought itt nott
fitt to stay where I had beene so injuriously traduced.   Therfore
to leave that familly I was fully resolved, butt where to goe I could
nott determine.

In all this time I had never heard nothing of C. B., nor from
him; wch had beene trouble enough to mee, had itt nott beene overcome by the presentt trouble I was in, wch made mee unsencible of
what was att a greater distance.   Butt noe sooner was I delivered
from ye sadness and discontentts occationed by what I have now
related, then a new misfortune arives. When I was hardly well composed affter one storme another rises, wch by the danger of others
involved mee by sympathy and gratitude in great disturbance. My
sister writtes me a long letter full of passion and discontentt, in-
forming mee that a cosen of her husband's, an heire to whom hee
was to succeed, was stollen away, and that affter much inquiry hee
heard that ye gentleman who had stollen her away had caried her to
Flanders, and that shee had fled to a monestary to secure her selfe

till my brother could come there to releeve her.　And unhapily in the same ship that hee wente over in C. B. was a passenger.　And though hee was disguised, yett my brother knew him, and as soone as they landed hee challenges him.　They chose their seconds, fights, and my brother was wounded in the hand so dangerously, that to loose the use of itt was the least that was expected.　How sadly this surprised mee is nott to bee imagined, for I should have been concerned in his misfortune though a stranger had occasioned itt.　Butt to thinke itt was upon my accountt, and done by one I was interested in, these considerations did highly agravate my trouble, and make mee conclude the same as my sister did in her letter, that I was the most unhapy person living, for I had nott only made my selfe so, butt brought misfortune upon all that related to mee.　Yett in the midst of all these disconsolations, I cannott butt accknowledge I had a sattisfaction to know so worthy a person as my brother N. owned a concerne for mee, wch hee would never have done (I was assured) if hee had beleeved mee vicious.

Within a litle while affter, C. B. sentt an exprese to mee, who was one of the persons who had assisted him in his escape, and could therfore give mee a true account of itt, and where hee was concealed till ye unhapy time of the incounter betwixt my brother N. and him. C. B. knew very well I could nott butt heare of itt, and that itt would very much afflict mee, and therfore hee writt a long letter in his owne vindication, and lest I should have a doupt of what hee said, he refferred the confirmation of itt to an inclosed letter directed to mee, written by the two seconds, and subscribed by them both, who had beene two colonells in the king's army.　My brother's second I cannott for the presentt remember his name, butt C. B.'s second was Co^{ll} Loe (who afterwards came into Scotland with the King). The account they gave was this.　When they were all fowre in the place apointed and there doubletts off, C. B., with his sword in his hand, came to my brother N. and told him hee was never ingaged in any imploymentt more contrary to his inclination than to make use of his sword against him who drew his in the deffence of the person hee loved beyond any living. That hee knew nott butt what hee was going now to say might bee ye last that ever hee should speake, and therfore as such hee desired to bee beleeved. Hee said hee did beleeve there was nott a more vertuous person in the world then I, nor did hee know his wife was living, and as this was true so hee desired the Lord to blese him in what hee was going aboutt. So they fight, and had severall passes withoutt advantage to either, butt my brother receaving a wound in his hand and bleeding fast, the seconds ran in and parted them, C. B. extreamly regretting what he had done, and my brother seeming to be sattisfied that hee had nott gott itt unhandsomely. This in short was the substance of there relation, wch they concluded with a great complement to mee. Though I never aproved of duells, yett if my prayers were heard for my brother's recovery I thought this would nott bee to my disadvantage.

Butt that wch pleased mee most was that C. B. had mett with my Lord Dunfermeline in Flanders (who, with other Commissioners were sentt from Scottland to invite his Majesty home), and aquainting his Lor^p. with what had beene betwixt him and mee, and justified himselfe as to what reports had beene made to his disadvantage, to obleige both him and mee, the Earle of Dunfermeline writt very earnestly to desire mee to come into Scotland, where the King intended to bee shortly, and therefore hee thought that would bee the most convenient time for mee to come, when I would have many freinds to asist mee for the recovery of my portion wch was in Scotch hands. C. B. seconded this with many arguments to perswade mee to hasten my journy all that was posible while the road was cleare, for there was reason to aprehend that Cromwell would soone march thither with the Army when hee heard the King was landed.

I showed my Lady H. my letters, and my resolution of obaying them; but my deficulty was how to undertake the journy, or live in a strange place, having litle or noe mony. Butt as to that my Lady H. very generously said I need nott trouble my selfe, for I should nott want what mony I desired, nor horses and men to

attend mee to Edenborough. I was nott then long determining of
the day for my departure. And Sr Charles apointed an old gentleman, a kinsman of his owne, with others, to bee ready to conduct
mee (and shee that served mee) att the time prefixed.

The night before I was to come away I sentt for Mr. N. and told
him hee should now have his desire in seeing mee outt of the house,
wch was what hee had used many unhandsome ways to bring aboutt;
and had itt nott beene for him itt is posible I had left that house
with more regrett. Now I was likely to bee att a great distance
from him, and therefore might expect hee would bee the more
liberall in his discourse of mee when I could nott vindicate myselfe.
" Butt (said I,) remember when ever you speake any thing to my disadvantage you are heard by the Allmighty God, who will plead for
mee, and your owne conscience (if you have one) will condemne you,
for you know I am inocentt of those unworthy things you charged
mee with." "I confese (replied hee,) there hath some unhapy circumstances fallen outt that may seeme to give you reason for what you
say. Butt I must suffer rather than vindicate myselfe to the prejudice of those under whose roofe I dwell ; butt if ever I am so hapy
as to see you outt of this familly, I shall then lett you see how much
you have beene mistaken of mee, and to evidence what my thoughts
are of you, I will give itt you under my hand that I do beleeve you
as vertuous a person as lives." I smiled att that, and with a dis-
dainefull looke told him my vertue would have butt a weake suport
if I had nothing to uphold itt butt a testimony from him. " Noe,
(said I,) I have a better hand to rely upon to defend mee, and such a
one as will make you ashamed for what you have done, except you
repentt. The respect I have to your calling, and the benefitt I have
had by your preaching and prayer, shall keepe mee from devulging
your faults ; butt, as you expect the Lord's blesing upon your
ministeriall office, and would avoid the beeing a scandall to itt,
leave off the course you have begun with mee; lest iff you practise
itt on any other itt may bring to remembrance ye injury you have

done mee, and so agravate your future crime." Affter I said this I
left him, and gave my Lady H. accountt of what I had said to him.

The next day I tooke my leave of my Lady and all the familly,
and S^r Ch. with a good attendance wentt part of the way; and none
in the familly butt gave some evidence of there concerne in parting
from mee except Mr. N., who hardly wentt to the gate with mee, and
for that was much censured by all, especially my Lady H. who had
great expresions of kindnese to mee, and said if that journy proved
unhapy to mee itt would bee a trouble to her as long as shee lived,
because shee was sure I had never undertaken itt so willingly if I
had nott beene disobleeged where I was. I could nott contradict so
great a truth, nor bee unsencible of her very great friendship, wch was
the more to bee valued because itt had mett with so strong a tryall,
and yett continued firme.

The second night affter I left N. Castle (Thursday, 6 June, 1650,)
I came to Edenborough, and lodged at Sainders Peeres, at the foott of
the Canongate. I had discharged all that were with mee to tell
my name to any one till I could find outt some that I had formerly
known in England. That night at super, the old gentleman beeing
with mee and the M^rs of the house, and siting fast against mee, I
could nott butt looke earnestly upon her, and I said, " Mrs. I
cannott butt have a kindnese for you, because you have a very great
resemblance of my mother." Att that shee clapt her hands, and said,
" Nay, then, I will never inquire any more who you are, for I am
sure you are Will Murray's sister, for hee often told mee ye same."
Shee then informed mee of a kinsman of my mother's (who shee
made her executor) that had beene at her house that day, and shee
knew hee would be glad to see mee. And I was well pleased to
hear of him, and sent for him to advise whether I should continue
where I was or take a more private lodging. Butt hee told mee it
was a very civill howse, and ye best quality lay there that had nott
howses of there owne.

When the gentleman and those that came with mee had rested

some time, and scene the towne, they returned back againe with all
the acknowlédgements I was capable to make to S^r Ch. and his
lady for there great civility and kindnese.

When I had béene two or three days in the towne I receaved a
visitt from the Earle of Argile, who invited mee to his howse, and
the next day sentt his coach for mee, wch I maid use of to waite
upon his lady. When I came up staires I was mett in the outtward
roome by my Lady Anne Campbell, a sight that I must confese did
so much surprise mee that I could hardly beleeve I was in Scottland,
for shee was very handsome, extreamely obleiging, and her behavier
and dress was equall to any that I had seene in the Court of England.
This gave mee so good impresions of Scottland, that I began to see
itt had beene much injured by those who represented itt under
another caracter then what I found itt. When I was brought in to
my Lady Argile I saw then where her daughter had derived her
beauty and civility ; one was under some decay, butt the other was
so evident and so well proportioned, that while shee gave to others
shee reserved what was due to her selfe.

Affter I had staid a convenientt time I returned home to my
lodging, where, amongst severall persons that visitted mee, S^r
James Dowglas came and earnestly invited mee to Aberdour to stay
some time with his Lady. Itt was too obleiging an offer to refuse,
and upon the 15. of June I wentt with him, and crosed att Leith to
Brun Island. As soone as I landed, Sr James Dowglas had mee by
one hand and the Laird of Maines by the other, and they bid mee
wellcome to Fife, and imediately I fell flat downe upon the ground,
and said, " I thinke I am going to take posesion of itt." They
blamed one another for having had so litle care of mee ; butt what I
thought then accidentall I have since looked upon as a presage of
ye future blesings I injoyed in Fife, for wch I shall for ever blese my
God, and the memory of that prostration shall raise in mee praise to
the Lord of bounty and mercy while I live.

When I came to Aberdour I was led in through the garden, w^{ch}
was so fragrant and delightfull that I thought I was still in England.

I intended to have staid there butt 2 or 3 nights, butt they would
nott part with mee till the 22. of June, and then I returned to Ed.,
butt wth a promise to bee backe againe, wch I made good the 27.
day.

Aboutt this time the news came that the King was landed in the
North, and was comming South. I began to reflect upon my owne
misfortune in ye unhapy report that was of C. B. wife's beeing alive,
and itt was knowne to severalls aboutt the Court what my concerne
in him was; this, with the unhandsome and unjust caracter given
both to him and my brother Will, made mee aprehend might make
mee nott bee so well looked upon by the King as otherways I
might expect. And therfore, to informe my selfe what reception I
should gett, I sentt an exprese to Mr. Seamar, who was one of the
grooms of the Bed Chamber, who had beene fellow servantt with
my brother Charles, and to him I writt representing the disadvantages I lay under, and that I expected his friendship in advising mee
whether I should goe to kisse the King's hand or forbeare, for I had
much rather wantt ye honor y^n receave itt with a frowne. To which
this was his answeare, dated from Faulkland, the 17. of July 1650:

"I shall have only time to tell you that his Matie saith that you
" shall bee very wellcome to him when soever you will give your-
" selfe that trouble, and that the world is too full of falce rumours
" easily to ingage his beleefe in any thing that shall bee to your
" prejudice ; and I am very confident, when you have spoken wth
" him, you will rest as assured of the esteeme that he hath of you
" as that I am, upon all occasions, your very humble servantt,

"H. SEYMOUR."

I was much sattisfied with this letter; and now my greatest
concerne was to find outt a convenientt time and place where
to performe my duty ; butt I was soone putt outt of that dispute by the Countess of Dunfermline, who came to Aberdour
to see her brother and his lady, and then told mee shee had
receaved a letter from her lord aquainting her what day the
King had determined to bee at Dunfermline (where his lordship

had invited his Matie), and injoyned her to give mee an invitation to bee there that day, as knowing noe place in Scottland I had more interest in, nor fitter for mee then there to attend the King. My lady was pleased to second her lord's desire with soe many obleiging expresions that I could nott in civility have denied to obay her commands, though itt had beene contrary to my inclination; butt knowing itt both my honour and advantage to be presentted to the King in that noble familly, I acknowledged the offer for a very great favor, and promised to wait upon her La^p. the day apointed; which I made good by the assistance of Sr James D. who wentt along with mee, and wee came to Dunfermeline some three houres before the King's arivall.

After his Matie had beene some time in ye bed-chamber reposing after the journy, I waited upon my Lady Dunfermeline and my Lady Anne Areskine to kisse the King's hand, beeing introduced by my Lord Argile and other persons of honour; and the first person I saw in ye bed-chamber was one of them who my brother Will had told mee was his enemy. I cannott butt accknowledge I was att first disordered when I saw him, and ye more that hee putt a question to mee to answeare wch I was obleiged either to dissemble or say what was very unfitt for the King to heare; butt I avoided both with that reason, because I was so neere, for the King heard my answeare and smiled. When I recollected the promise I had made my brother to forgive that person, and never to quarrell with him for the injury hee had done him, I so farre made itt good that I had an opertunity y^t with much ease and unknowne I could have had him putt from ye court att that time when many were dismissed that had come home with ye King; for a person who had great influence upon those who then governed inquired of mee particularly concerning him, of whom I gave so favourable a caracter that hee was continued to attend his Matie.

During the time the King continued at Dunfermeline, wch was 8 or ten days, beeing royally intertained by the Earle of Dunferme-line, and all those who attended his Matie, every day I waited upon my lady and her neece when they wentt to attend the King either att dinner or super; and though att those times hee was pleased to looke faverably upon mee, yett itt was noe more then what hee did to strangers. This did much trouble mee; and therfore the day before the King was to goe from Dumfermcline I sentt for Mr. Harding in the morning to my chamber, and told him, though my aquaintance with him was butt of a short date, yett for the friend-ship I heard hee had for my brother Charles, who was his fellow servantt, I made choice of him whose age and experience might make more sencible (of what I could nott butt regrett) then those whose youth made them unconcerned in any trouble that was nott there owne. I then vindicated my brother Will from the aspersion hee lay under, and wch I am confidentt occationed his death; and representted my owne misfortune, wch posibly I might have avoided if I had not ingaged in serving his Highnese the Duke of Yorke in his escape, many circumstánces attending that having contributed to my presentt suffering both as to my fame and fortune: for, beeing necesitate to leave London for my owne security, itt was easy for the malicious to deprive mee of both when I was nott in a capacity to speake in my owne defence. "And affter all this (said I,) itt is an agravation of my trouble to see the King never take notice of mee, wch may bee a great discouragementt to those persons of honor who have beene very civill to mee to continue so when they see mee so litle regarded by his Matie." I could nott utter this without teares, in wch the good old gentleman did keepe mee company, expresing a very great respect for mee, and promised to speake to the King, and give an accountt of what I had said.

The next day, presenttly affter the King had dined, when his Matie had taken leave of my Lady Dunfermcline and given her a complementt and my Lady Anne Areskine (her lord's neece), hee came to mee and said, "Mrs. Murray, I am ashamed I have been so long a' speaking to you, butt itt was because I could nott say enough to you for the service you did my brother; butt if ever I can com-mand what I have right to as my owne, there shall bee nothing in my power I will nott doe for you;" and with that the King laid his hand upon both mine as they lay upon my breast. I humbly bowed down and kist his Maties hand, and said I had done nothing butt my duty, and had recompense enough if his Matie accepted of itt as a service, and allowed mee his faver. Affter some other discourse wch I have forgot, the King honored mee with the farwell hee had given the ladys, and imediately wentt to horse.

As soone as the King parted from mee, there came two gentlemen to mee; one tooke mee by one hand, the other by the other, to lead mee outt to the court (where all the ladys wentt to see the King take horse,) with so many flattering expresions that I could nott butt with a litle disdaine tell them I thought they acted that part very well in *The Humourous Lieutenant*, where a stranger comming to see a solemnity was hardly admitted to looke on by those who afterwards troubled her with there civility when they saw the King take notice of her. This answeare putt them both a litle outt, and made them know I understood their humour.

To allay the joy that all the loyall party had for the King's returne, there was two great occasions for disturbance, the one beeing strenghened by the other: Cromwell comming in with an army when there was so great devissions both in Church and State, and such unsuitable things proposed for accomodation as I wish were buried in perpetuall silence.

Affter the King had been invited to severall places and intertained suitably to what could bee expected, his Matie returned againe to Dunfermeline, having ordered ye forces to march; and one morning came letters from ye army lying att Dunbar that they had so surrounded the enemy that there was noe posibility for them to escape, wch news gave great joy and much security. Butt the sad effects made us see how litle confidence should bee placed in any thing butt God, who in his justice thought fitt to punish this kingdome and bring itt under subjection to an Usurper, because they paid nott that subjection that was due to there lawfull King. The unexpected defeat wch the King's army had at Dunbar putt every one to new thoughts how to dispose of themselves, and none was more perplexed than I where to goe or what to doe. Againe my Lady Dunfermeline invited mee to goe North with her La^p., assuring mee of much wellcome and that I should fare as shee did, though shee could nott promise any thing butt disorder from so sodaine a removall to a howse that had nott of a long time had an inhabitantt. I had much reason to accept of this offer with more than an ordinary sence of God's goodnese; for there could nott have beene a more seasonable act of generosity than this to a stranger that was destitute of all meanes that should asist mee in a retreat. I sentt my woman over to Ed., and writt to a lady who I had knowne from my infancy att London, and another letter to the gentleman who was my mother's executor, and from both I desired to borow what mony they could conveniently spare. I named the sum I desired from the lady, wch shee very friendly sentt upon the note of my hand; butt my cousin excused himselfe, because hee had itt nott of his owne, butt said hee had spoken to Sr G. S. who had promised to lend mee 25*l.* sterling upon my note, which hee made good, and then I was the better sattisfied to waite upon my Lady Dunfermeline to the North, when I was provided so with mony as that I should bee the less troublesome to her La^p.

1650. Upon Satturday the 7. of September wee left Dunfermeline, and came that night to Kinrose, where wee staid till Monday. I cannott omitt to insert here the opertunitty I had of serving many poor wounded soldiers, for as wee were riding to Kinrose I saw two that looked desperately ill, who were so weake they were hardly able to goe along the high way; and inquiring what ailed them, they told mee they had beene soldiers att Dunbar, and were going towards Kinrose if there wounds would suffer them. I bid y^m when they came there inquire for ye Countess of D. lodging, and there would bee one there would drese them. Itt was late itt seemes before they came, and so till ye next morning I saw them nott, butt then they came attended with twenty more, and betwixt that time and Monday that wee left that place I beleeve threescore was the least that was

dresed by mee and my woman and Ar. Ro. who I imployed to such
as was unfitt for mee to drese; and besides the plaisters or balsam
I aplied, I gave every one of them as much with them as might
drese them 3 or 4 times, for I had provided myselfe very well of
things nesesary for that imploymentt, expecting they might bee
usefull.   Amongst the many variety of wounds amongst them two
was extreordinary : one was a man whose head was cutt so that the
(*blank*) was very visibly seene, and the watter came bubbling
up, wch when Ar. R. saw hee cried outt, " Lord have mercy upon
thee! for thou art butt a dead man." I seeing the man who had
courage enough before begin to bee much dishartened, I told him
hee need nott bee discouraged with whatt hee that had noe skill
said, for if itt pleased God to blese what I should give him hee
might doe well enough; and this I said more to harten him up
than otherways, for I saw itt a very dangerous wound; and yett itt.
pleased God hee recovered, as I heard affterwards, and wentt frankly
from dresing, having given him something to refresh his spiritts.
The other was a youth aboutt 16 that had beene run through the
body with a tuke.   Itt wentt in under his right shoulder and came
outt under his left breast, and yett [he] had litle inconvenience by
itt; butt his greatest prejudice was from so infinitt a swarme of crea-
tures that itt is incredible for any that were nott eye-wittneses of itt.
I made a contribution and bought him other cloaths to putt on
him, and made ye fire consume what els had beene unposible to dis-
troy. Of all these poore soldiers there was few of them had ever beene
drest from the time they receaved there wounds till they came to
Kinrose, and then itt may bee imagined they were very noisome ;
butt one particularly was in that degree who was shott through the
arme that none was able to stay in ye roome, butt all left mee.
Accidentally a gentleman came in, who seeing mee (nott withoutt
reluctancy) cutting off the man's sleeve of his doublet, wch was
hardly fitt to be toutched, hee was so charitable as to take a knife
and cutt itt off and fling [it] in ye fire.

    When I had dresed all that came, my Lady D. was by this time

ready to goe away, and came to St Johnston that night, where the
King and Court was. My La. A. A. and I waited upon my Lady
into her sister the C. of Kinowle, and there my Lord Lorne came to
mee, and told mee that my name was offten before the Councell that
day. I was much surprised, wch his Lor^p. seeing kept mee ye longer
in suspense ; att last hee smiling told mee there was a gentleman
(wch itt scemes was hee that had cutt off the man's sleeve) that had
given the King and Councell accountt of what hee had seene and
heard I had done to the poore soldiers, and representing the sad
condittion they had beene in withoutt y^t relcefe, there was pre·
senttly an order made to apoint a place in severall townes, and chi-
rugions to have allowance for taking care of such wounded soldiers
as should come to them. And the King was pleased to give mee
thanks for my charity. I have made this relation because itt was
the occation of bringing mee much of the devertissements I had in a
remotter place.

Upon Thursday night the 19. of September my Lady Dunfermeline kist the King's hands, and tooke leave of all her relations in
St Johnston to goe on her journy to Fivye. The first night wee
lay att Glames, the next two nights att Brighon, upon Monday
night att Donotter, the next night att Aberdeene, where wee
staid till Friday the 27., and that night came to Fivye, where
I was intertained with so much respect and civility both by my
Lady Dunfermeline and my Lady Anne Ariskene, and the whole
familly, that I shall ever acknowledge itt with all the gratitude
imaginable.

Affter I had beene there some time the King came to Aberdeene,
and my Lord D. came home for a weeke to see his Lady, and told
mee that Sr G. S. had desired his Lordship to lett mee know that
some friends of his was to present the King with a purse with gold,
and if I would imploy any that I had interest in to speake to the
King for mee, hee doupted nott butt his Matie would give mee part
of the presentt. When my Lord returned I writt of itt to Mr.
Seamor, and att the first proposall the King was pleased to give

order for sending fivety pieces to mee Halfe of itt I paid to the gentleman that had formerly lentt itt mee, who had found this way to secure himselfe and obleige mee, and so I was free of that dept to my very greatt sattisfaction.

I had nott beene long injoying the tranquility of that retired condittion I was in when I received a letter from C. B. that hee was att Aberdeene, and desired to know if hee might have liberty to come and see mee att Fivye. I was altogether averse to itt, and used many argumentts to diswade him from itt, beeing positively determined nott to see him till hee could free himselfe of what hee was taxed with; for, though I did nott beleeve itt, and that hee had so fully sattisfied my Lord Dun. in Holland that his Lor⁰ (as hee often told mee) had nott the least doupt of itt, yett I thought the safest way was to keepe att a distance till itt was past dispute. Hee so offten importuned mee that att last hee prevailed, and, having aquainted my Lady Dunfermeline with his desire, and obtained her Laˢ liberty, I gave my consentt; butt while the question was in debate the King returned towards Sterling, and hee attending (as the rest did) his Maᵗⁱᵉ, itt tooke up a considerable time before my answeare could come to him, and hee come to Fivye. Butt affter I had despatched his foot-boy I began to have great debates with my selfe, and the conflict betwixt love and honor was so great and prevalent that neither would yield to other, and betwixt both I was brought into so great a distemper that I expected now an end to all my misfortunes; butt itt seemes the Lord had some further use for mee in the world, and therfore thought fitt then againe to spare mee. What yᵉ trialls were that I mett with under that sicknese are knowne to some yett living, and the submission under them was, I hope, acceptable to him that gave itt.

Before I recovered so much strengh as to be able to sitt up, C. B. came, whose sattisfaction in seeing mee was much abated to find mee so weake, and for seeming so douptfull of the reports concerning him; and since what hee had said to my brother N. (when hee thought itt might have beene the last moment of his life,) did nott sattisfy mee, hee offred to take the most holy sacramentt upon itt that hee was inocentt if itt should bee true that his wife was living, and gave so many reasons why itt should nott bee true that I could nott butt accknowledge pleaded much for him.   I alltogether dis- allowed of making use of that sacred institution for the end hee proposed, since I did nott thinke itt warrantable, nor could itt con- vince mee of the untruth of the report, though itt might confirme hee was inocentt of itt; and that charity inclined mee to beleeve, for hee could expect noe advantage with mee to countervaile the con- trivance of so ill a designe ; and I thought noe person could bee so ill as doe what's sinfull merely because itt is a sin, and therfore I concluded either the report falce, or hee miserably abused as well as I.   Affter hee had staid two nights hee tooke his leave of mee, having assured mee ever to keepe a due distance with him till the truth were evidentt beyond any one's contrediction ; and if I found hee had been injured, hee might bee confidentt noe other missfortune under heaven should separate mee from him when ever I found I might lawfully and conveniently make good what I had designed.

Itt would bee too tedious to relate here how I spentt ye time I was att Fyvie, wch was neere two yeares ; butt itt was so agre- ably that in all my life I never was so long together so truly con- tented; for the noble familly I was in dayly increased my obligation to them, and the Lord was pleased to blese what I gave to the helpe of the sicke and wounded persons came to mee, part of them from Kinrose; and some English soldiers came to try my charity, wch I did nott deny to them, though they had itt nott withoutt exhorting them to repentt there sin of rebellion and become loyall.   The variety of distempered persons that came to mee was nott only a devertissmentt, butt a helpe to instruct mee how to submit under my owne croses, by seeing how patient they were under thers, and yett some of them intollerable by wanting a sence of faith, wch is ye greatest suport under afflictions.   There was three most remarkeable of any that came to mee: one, Isbell Stevenson, who had beene three yeare under a discomposed spiritt ; the other was a young woman who

had beene very beautyfull, and her face became loathsomely deformed
with a cancerous humour that had overspread itt, wch deprived her
of her nose and one of her eyes, and had eaten much of her forhead
and cheecks away; the third was a man that had a horne on the left
side of the hinder part of his head, betwixt 4 and 5 inches aboutt
and two inches long, and his wife told mee shee had cutt the lengh
of her finger off (as shee usually did) when two or three days before
hee came to mee, because the weight of itt was troublesome. A
further accountt of these may bee had hereaffter iff itt bee necesary.

The misfortune in the King's affaires gave his enemys the greater
advantage, and was a discouragementt to the loyall party to see how
succesfull Cromwell's army was, who now marched where they
pleased, and gave laws to the whole kingdome. The Earle of D.
beeing left behind the King (when his Matie marched into England)
with others of the Councell to order what was fitt to be done in his
Maties absence, they were soone putt from acting any thing, and
was forced to suffer what they could nott preventt. Butt as long
as they had any retreat they still retired to bee outt of there
enemys hands; and my Lord D. came to Fyvie, and when the Army
came to Aberdeene hee wentt to Muray till hee could make some
capitulation for himselfe; for when noe resistance could bee made,
the next remedy was to make as good condittions as every one could
for themselves.

The Army comming now towards Fyvie, some scattering soldiers
came in there who had noe officer butt one they made amongst
themselves, and called him Major. When they came into the
howse they were very rude, beating all the men came in there way,
and frighting the weemen, and threatening to pistoll who ever
did nott give what they called for. My Lady Dunfermeline, beeing
then great with child, was much disordered with feare of their inso-
lence, and with teares in her eyes desired mee to goe and speake to
them, to see if I could prevaile with them as beeing their country
woman, butt (says shee,) I know nott well how to desire itt, because
I heare they say they are informed there is an English woman in

the howse, and if they get her they will be worse to her then any.
" Madam, (said 1,) if my going to them can doe your La^s service, I
will take my hazard, and had gone to them before, butt that I
thought itt nott fitt for mee in your La^s howse to take upon mee to
say any thing to them till I had your La^s command for itt." Then
calling my woman I wentt downe where they were, and being instructed which was the major (as they called him), who ordered y^e
rest as hee pleased (and I beleeve gott that authority by humouring
them in all they desired), I made my adrese first to him, beleeving
if I prevailed with him the rest were soone gained. As soone as I
came amongst them, the first question they asked mee was if I were
the English whore that came to meet the King, and all sett their
pistolls just against mee. (I had armed myselfe before by seeking
assistance from Him who only could protect mee from there fury,
and I did so much rely upon itt that I had nott the least feare, tho
naturally I am the greatest coward living.) I told them I owned
myselfe to bee an English woman and to honor the King, butt for
the name they gave mee I abhorred itt; butt my comming to them
was nott to dispute for my selfe, butt to tell them I was sorry to
heare that any of the English nation, who was generally esteemed
the most civill people in the world, should give so much occation to
be thought barbarously rude, as they had done since there comming
into the howse, where they found none to resist them, but by the
contrary whatever they called for, either to themselves or horses, was
ordered by my Lady to bee given them. " What advantage (said I,)
can you propose to yourselves to fright a person of honor who is great
with child, and few butt chilldren and weemen in the howse?
and if by your disorder any misfortune hapen to my Lady, or any
belonging to the familly, you may expect to be called to an accountt
for itt, because I am very confidentt you have no allowance from your
officers to be uncivill to any, and I am sure itt is more your interest
to obleege all you can then to disobleege them, for the one will
make you loved, the other hated; and judge which will be most for
your advantage." They heard mee with much patience; and att last

flinging downe there pistolls upon the table, the major gave mee his
promise that neither hee nor any with him should give the least disturbance to the meanest in the familly, only desired meatt and drinke
and what was nesesary that they called for ; and they did so keepe
there word that my L. Dunfermeline was by there staying in the howse
secured from many insoleneys that were practised in other places.

A litle affter there came to Fyvie three regimentts with there
officers, beeing commanded by Coll. Lilburne, Coll. Fitts, and Co.
Overton. My Lady D. inquired of mee, when shee heard they were
comming, if I knew any of those, because shee would desire mee if
I did to gett a pass for my Lord D. to have liberty to returne home.
I said I had only seene Coll. Fitts when I was at N. Castle, butt had
never spoken to him, and if hee owned the knowledge of mee I
would then indeavour to serve her La⁸, butt if nott I would speake
to those I had never seene rather than him. When they all came up
to the dining roome, and saluted my Lady D. and my L. A. Arisken,
when Coll. Fitts came to salute mee, hee lifted up his hands as
beeing astonished to see mee there, and came to mee with the
greatest joy hee could exprese, and taking mee by the hand said to
my Lady Dun. " Madam, I must beg liberty to speake with Mʳˢ M.
and give her accountt of her freends in England." So hee and I
sat downe together att some distance from the rest, and hee gave
mee a relation of all yᵗ had hapened in N. Castle affter my comming
away; some things that I was sory for, even for Mr. N., who itt
seemes had nott followed my advice, butt traducing a person (who
came there presently affter I wentt away) who could nott suffer itt
as I had done, butt tooke a revenge suitable enough to the fault,
though unsuitable to one of his function. And I cannott omitt to
remarke that itt was performed in the garden nott farre from the
place where hee so confidently denyed a truth, wᶜʰ I hope, beeing
punished there, made him reflect upon his sin and made him penitentt for itt; and I have reason nott only to forgive him, butt to
thanke him for the injury hee did mee, since the Lord turned itt to
my advantage.

When I found Coll. Fitts thus free and civill, offring mee any service in his power, I told him how much hee would obleige my Lady D., who was now neere her time, if hee would give a pass for my Lord to returne; wch hee promised, and made good when hee came to Elgin, where my Lord was, for hee wentt to him and prevented his Lor^s seeking anything by making offer of all hee could desire.

That day the officers wentt away, Coll. Overton sitting by mee at dinner, said to mee that God had wonderfully evidenced his power in the great things hee had done. I replied, noe doupt butt God would evidence his power still in the great things hee designed to doe. I spoke this with more than ordinary earnestnese, wch made him say, " You speake my words, butt nott I thinke to my sence." " When I know y^r sence, (said I,) then I will tell you whether itt bee mine or noe." " I speake (said hee,) of the wonderfull workes that God hath done by his servantts in the late times, that are beyond what any could have brought aboutt withoutt the imediate assistance of God, and his derection." " S^r, (said I,) if you had nott begun this discourse, I had said nothing to you; butt since you have desired my opinion (wch hee did) of the times, I shall very freely give itt, upon the condittion that what ever I say you may nott make use of itt to the prejudice of the noble familly I live in, for I can hold my toung, butt I cannott speake any thing contrary to what I thinke. I cannott butt confese you have had great success in all your undertakings ; butt y$^{t's}$ noe good rule to justify ill actions. You pretend to great zeale in relligion, and obedience to God's words. If you can shew mee in all the Holy Scriptures a warrant for murdering your lawfull King and banishing his posterity, I will then say all y^u have done is well, and will bee of your opinion; butt as I am sure that cannott bee done, so I must condemne that horid act, and whatever is done in prosecution of itts vindication." Hee replied, that those who had writt upon the prophesy of Daniell showed y^t hee foretold the distruction of monarky many yeares since, and that itt was a tiranicall governmentt, and therfore fitt to be destroyed. " How comes (said I,) you have taken the power

from y⁰ Parliamentt and those succesive interests that have
governed since you wanted the King?" "Because (said hee,) wee
found affter a litle time they began to bee as bad as hee, and therfore wee changed." "And (said I,) so you will ever find reason to
change what ever governmentt you try till you come to beg of the
King to come home and governe you againe; and this I am as confident of as I am speaking to you." "If I thought that would bee
true, (replied hee,) I would repentt all that I have done." "Itt will
come to that I dare assure you, (said I,) and the greatest hinderance
will bee that you thinke your crimes have beene such as is imposible
hee should forgive you; butt to incourage you I can assure you that
there never was any prince more inclined to pardon, nor more easy
to be intreated to forgive." "Well, (says hee,) if this should come
to pass, I will say you are a prophetess." Here wee broke off,
because wee saw the rest of the table take notice of our seriousnes.
I found affterwards hee was nott unsattisfied with my discourse, for
hee came severall times to see mee when I came to Ed^b, and remembred many things I had said to him wch I have now forgott.

When the whole kingdome was now brought under the bondage
of the Usurper, and finding noe remedy butt to submitt till the Lord
thought fitt to give them deliverance, every one thought now of
returning where there interest led them; and my Lord Dunfermeline having beene att Fyvie some time, and staid till his lady was
delivered of her daughter my Lady Henrietta, and mending againe,
his Lor^s resolved to goe to Ed^b aboutt his affaires, and I thought
itt would bee a convenientt time for mee to returne then with his
Lord^s; butt hee having first some occation to goe to Elgin, my
curiosity to see that country made mee prevaile wth my Lady Anne
Areskine to goe with her unckle, and lett mee waite upon her to
Murray. Wee wentt from Fyvie Wednesday the 2nd of June,
1652, and crosed the river Spey att the Boge ; upon Friday
came backe againe to Garmuth, and crosed there the next day,
and came home by Fordice to Fyvie. Though I was resolved of my
journy to Eden^b, yett I was much troubled how to performe itt,

for my mony was neere spentt, and having beene so long a trouble
to my Lady D. I had nott the confidence to seeke to borrow any
for carrying mee South. Many deficultys in ye way represented
themselves to mee, and what I might meett with att Ed^b, and
my woman was weeping by mee as beeing much discouraged with
the inconveniences shee aprehended I might bee exposed to. I
smiled upon her, and bid her have a good hart, for though my presentt coudittion seemed very darke and cloudy, yett I was confidentt
I should see a sun-shyny day, for though I was now incompased
round with misfortunes, yett I was very sure I should bee as hapy
as I could desire, though I could nott tell wch way itt would come
to pase; and for my presentt suplys I would rely upon God, who
had never yett left mee in my greatest deficultys, and to his direction I resigned myselfe, beeing confidently asured hee would provide some unexpected meanes to free mee of my presentt trouble;
and with that conclusion I wentt to bed with as quiett repose as if
I had had nothing to disturbe mee.

The next morning early the midwife (who had come from Dal-
keith to my Lady) came into my chamber with her riding-cloaths on
to take her leave of mee, and said shee had a request to mee before
shee wentt, wch was (hearing that I intended to bee att Ed^b shortly)
that I would doe her the favor to take the mony shee had gott from
my Lady and others att the christening, and bring itt South wth mee,
because shee durst take noe more with her then her expences by the
way because shee aprehended beeing plundered by the soldiers. I
told her iff shee thought itt secure with mee, I would doe her that
courtesy, and deliver itt where shee would apoint att Ed^b. So I receaved itt from her, and gave her a note of my hand for itt, beeing
aboutt ten pound sterling, and shee wentt away very well pleased,
butt litle knew how much more reason shee had given mee to be so,
for I looked nott on itt only as a presentt advantage, butt as a recompense for the reliance I had upon my most gracious God, and an
incouragementt still to do so.

Itt was noe wonder if I had trouble to part with the noble familly at Fyvie, where I had beene neere two yeare treated with all the kindnese imaginable, and where my sattisfaction was so great that I could contentedly have spentt the remainder of my life there if itt had beene as convenientt as itt was pleasing. Butt now itt was time to free my Lady of the trouble I had given her so long, and nesesary for mee to goe to Edin[b] to looke affter what was my concerne, and to begin a law suite for recovering y[e] most considerable part of my portion. So having taken my leave of my Lady and my L. A. Ariskine and all the familly, nott with dry eyes of either side (butt y[e] teares that moved mee most was from that good old man Mr. George Sharpe, Minister of Fyvie, and his wife, to and from whom I gave and receaved much respect), upon Thursday y[e] 24. of June, 1652, my Lord Dunfermeline, with his nephew the late Lord Lyon and severall other gentlemen, wentt from Fyvie, allowing mee and my woman the honour of there company, and lay that night att my Lord Frazer's att Mohull, the next night att Northwatter brig, a' Saturday night att Belcarese, where wee staid till Tuesday; that night came to Brunt Island; and Wednesday the 30. to Ed[b], where I wentt to my former lodging att Sainders Speers, and staid there some time till S[r] Robert Muray and his lady came to towne, who lying att the Neither Bow perswaded mee to take a chamber neere them, which was an advantage nott to be refused, having allso the conveniency of beeing neerer the place where all my busynese chiefely lay. The lodging they chused for mee was up the staires by John Meenes shop, belonging to a discreet old gentlewoman, who had a backe way up to the roomes shee used her selfe.

I had nott beene there two or three nights, when, my Lord Dunfermeline and my Lord Belcarese having supt with mee, and gone away aboutt 9 a' clocke, I sate up later than ordinary to write letters to Fyvie with one going there the next morning, and before I had quite done there came soldiers to the chamber doore and knockt very rudely. Att first I made y[m] noe answeare, butt they knockt with that violence that I thought they would have broke up the door, and y[n] I inquired who they were, and what they

would have. They told mee they would come in and see who was
with mee, or what I was doing. I told them I knew noe warrantt
they had for that inquiry, yett to sattisfy them I assured them there
was none there butt myselfe and my woman. They told mee I lyed,
and that if I would nott open ye doore they would breake itt open.
I knew nott what to say or doe, butt I bid Crew (which was my
woman's name) goe and desire the M^{rs} of the howse to come downe.
They hearing the backe doore open, cried outt, " Shee hath now lett
them outt att ye backe doore; goe and stope them;" and with that
they forced up the doore and run through the roome, and some
wentt up staires and some downe the staires, butt finding noe body
they came in in a great chafe. I asked them if they had found
those they wentt to seeke. They said Noe, for I had lett them outt.
" Gentlemen, (said I,) you may assure yourselves I will complaine of
you to your officers, for if I may nott have liberty in my owne
lodging to sitt up and burne a candle as long as I please without
having such a disturbance, and upon such unworthy grounds as you
would inferre, I thinke few will heare of itt that will nott condemne
your uncivill actions." They seemed to justify themselves by an
order they said they had to breake up any doores where they saw
lights affter ten a' clocke, and that they had beene civill, and expected I would give them something to drinke. I told them when
they deserved itt they should have itt; butt sure they could nott
expect itt from mee, having done as much as they could to bring a
scandall upon mee that was a stranger newly come there, and therfore might bee the greater prejudice. They saw mee very angry,
and that they could nott prevaile to get anything, and therfore left
mee in disorder enough to thinke what the neibours aboutt might
think of mee to heare what they said and did at my chamber doore.
The next morning I sentt for W. Muray of Hermiston, who was
very great with ye English officers, and desired him to goe to their
captaine and complaine, wch hee did, and there captaine sentt downe
to referre to mee there punishmentt, for they had noe allowance for
what they did. I soone remitted there punishmentt, condittionally
that they did nott practice the like againe. The noise of this came

to as many persons' cares as I was aquainted with, and the disorder
I was in by aprehending itt might bee usuall to have such alarums
as long as I lay there, having a great window to the strectt, and
none in ye howse butt weemen, this made mee thinke of changing
my lodging. butt where to fixe I was undetermined, when my Lord
Twedale and my Lady very oblicgingly offred mee the use of some
roomes in his Lord^s howse, they beeing y^n to goe outt of towne,
and left only one roome furnished, and a porter to take care of the
howse. I accepted of the offer with very great sence of the faver,
butt my next deficulty was where to borow or hire furniture for my
chamber and my woman's. That wantt was withoutt my seeking
supplied by my Lady Belcarese, who very civilly lent mee all nesesary accomodations. So I removed my lodging into my Lord
Twedale's howse, wch I had never had the offer of if the insolency
of the soldiers had nott given occation for itt; and so I had an
advantage by ye prejudice they intended mee.

Affter I had beene some time setled I inquired for Mr. W. H., who
was the lawyer who (in my mother's life time had upon her asignation
to mee of ye bond of 2000l. sterling, with interest from '47) began
the suite in my name against Ar. Hay who was caution for that sum
with the E. of Kinowle. A. Hay beeing now dead, I was to proceed
against his executors. What the trouble and expense of that pro-
cese was is too tedious to relate here, butt in gratitude I shall ever
accknowledge the obligation I had to my Lord Newbeth and his father,
who I could never perswade to take one peny of mee, and yett they
were as ready to asist mee with there advice and attendance to
solicitte the judges as they who tooke most from mee. The great
disadvantage I had was, that my antagonist was very favourably
looked upon by the English judges as beeing inclined to there
principles, and they looked upon mee as a Malignantt, and therefore
they gave him all the advantage hee could desire against mee, w^{ch}
was by delays, while hee secured himselfe by fraudulent conveyencys
of all the mony in good hands, and then they gave mee a decreet for
recovering the rest. What I have now related in few words cost

mee some yeares attendance. Butt I shall leave what relates to that
to mention some other particulars more to my sattisfaction.

After I had beene some time at my Lord Tweedale's howse, one
Thursday my Lord Dunfermeline came to see mee, and brought a
gentleman with him who I had never scene before, and told mee
they had beene both dining with my Lady Morton, who was going
to Sir John Gilmour's lady's buriall, and had promised to call y^m,
and they had only so much time as to come in and aske how I
liked my new lodging.   I had scarce gieven an answeare when one
came in to tell mee Mr. D. Dickson was without. I wentt to y^e
doore to bring him in, butt cheefely to aske one of my Lord D.
servantts what gentleman that was with his Lord, who told mee itt
was Sr James Halkett. I said, " If hee had nott come with your
Lord, I would nott have beene so civill as I am to him, because hee
hath a sword aboutt him;" for all the nobility and gentry had that
marke of slavery upon them that none had liberty to weare a sword,
only such as served there interest and disowned the King, wch made
mee hate to see a Scotch man with a sword. Mr. Seaton, who I
was speaking to, smiled and said I was mistaken, for itt was only a
sticke hee held in his hand under his coate, that stucke outt like a
sword, for hee was too honest a gentleman to weare one now.
Going in againe and seeing my error made mee change my thoughts
of him.   Presently after word came that my Lady Morton staid in
her coach for them at ye doore, and they wentt away. This was the
first time I saw S^r Ja. Halkett; butt before Saturday night I had
five visitts from him, every time making a severall pretence, either
inquiring for Sir Robert Muray or my Ld D., or bringing some
commission to mee from my Lady Morton. Hee was cousin german
with Sr R. M. and much respected and very intimate with the
other, and therefore I could nott butt bee very civill to him upon
that accountt; and I saw noe reason butt that hee might challenge
itt upon his owne.

After I had beene some time in Ed^b, I had a visitt from one who
had frequently beene at my mother's, and was much obleiged to a

neere relation of mine, and to them [him ?] I told the deficulty I had to gett any mony outt of England, and the few I had interest in to borow of in Ed[b], and hee very civilly lentt mee what paid the mony w[ch] the midwife trusted to my care, and for other nesesary occations.

Beeing now setled, and putt my affaires in such hands as would bee carefull of them in my absence, I resolved to goe into England and see my Lady H., having the conveniency of horses lentt mee by my Lord Dunfermeline's mother, who was extreamly obleiging to mee, and the more because shee knew I was a faithfull servantt to all that owned the King's interest, for shee was an extreordinary Royallist. Beeing provided with all things for my journy, and intending to goe first to the Fleurs, where I was invited by the Countese of Roxbery, to hasten my journy I receaved a letter from C. B., writt in cipher, giving mee accountt that affter many hazards and deficultys hee was come to the North of England, where hee staid privately till hee could inquire where I was, and that I could advise him where hee might speake with S[r] R. Moray. I gave him an answeare by the same way I receaved his, and aquainted him with my intention of going to N. Castle, and apointed a day that I intended to bee att Anwicke, where, if hee durst venture to come, I should then lett him know S[r] R. Moray's opinion of the fittest place for to meett with him, for I had told S[r] R. my designe, and had his aprobation.

When I was come to y[e] Fleurs, and staid there two or three days, I wentt on my intended journy towards N. Castle ; but when I came to Anwicke C. B. diswaded mee from going there, because there was some there that I was nott desirous to see, and so I returned backe again the next day and came to the Fleurs, where I staid till Crew came backe, who I sentt to N. Castle to bringe my trunkes and what I had left there for wantt of conveniency to bring them with my selfe (when I came from thence). The intertainment I had att the Fleurs was so agreeable that I had noe reason to bee weary the time I was there ; nor was I unsattisfied to returne to

Ed^b, because C. B. was uncertaine how to dispose of himselfe till hee heard againe from mee. I gave Sr R. M. and my Lord D. an accountt of his designs, wch was to waite all opertunitys wherein hee might serve the King, and if there were any probability of doing itt in Scottland, hee would then come there and hazard his life as farre as any could propose itt to bee rattionall. The advice they gave was to conceale himselfe where hee was for some time till they saw a fitt opertunity to invite him to Ed^b, where they beleeved hee might bee secure enough, since hee was knowne to very few there butt such as was his friends. While hee continued in the North of England I heard frequently from him, and still gave him accountt of what hopes or feares there was of acting anything for ye King, which I had the more opertunity to doe because my chamber was the place where Sr Robert M. most commonly mett with such persons as were designing to serve the King. Amongst the rest, Sr James H. sel-dome missed to be one.

Sr R. M.'s lady beeing great with child, and having noe conve-nient lodging where shee used to lye, desired some roomes in my L^d. Tweedalls howse, which his Lord. readily granted, to my very great sattisfaction, for I could nott desire the converse of any person more for my advantage; for shee was devoutly good without show or affectation, extreamly pleasing in discourse, civill to all, and of a constant cheerfull humour. Wee allways eate together, and seldome asunder any other part of the day except for convenient retirements; and though that howse was the rendezvous of the best and most loyall when they came to towne, yett none was so constantly there as Sr James H.; and though his relation to Sr Robert was ground enough for his frequentt beeing there, yett any that saw him in my company could nott butt take notice that hee had a more then ordi-nary respect for mee, which though I thought myself obleeged to him for, yett itt was a great trouble to mee, since I was nott in a capacity to give him such a returne as hee might expect or deserve; and, to preventt his declaring to mee what was visible enough, I resolved to give him an opertunity of beeing in my chamber alone

wth mee (wch before I had much avoided), that I might putt an end
to his beeing further concerned in mee. When hee came in and
was sett downe, aftter some generall discourse, I told him I had
beene very much obleiged to his civility ever since I knew him,
and I looked upon him as so worthy a person that I could nott conceale from him the greatest concerne I had, and my greatest misfortune, wch was that when I had ingaged my selfe to a person who I
was fully determined to marry, my brother and sister, to diswade
mee from itt, found noe motive so strong as to indeaver to perswade
mee that I was abused in beleeving his wife was dead, for shee was
alive; and because I did rather beleeve him then they, this occationed there unkindnese. "You may beleeve (said I,) such a report
could nott butt make me thinke my selfe extreamely unhapy; butt
those whose judgmentts I rely upon more then my owne, as Sr R. M.
and my Lord Dun. who hath spoke with him, and are so fully convinced that he is injured, that they chide mee when I seeme to
have the least doupt of itt. Now, S^r, (said I,) this relation may
confirme I have a great confidence of your friendship when I trust
you with this, and doe intend when hee comes here, wch I shortly
expect, to presentt him to you as one that I hope you will nott
beleeve unworthy your knowledge." This discourse did strangely
surprise him, butt hee indeavored to hide his disorder as well as hee
could, and said hee was sory for my brother's unkindnese, and if
hee were neere him hee would indeavour to reconcile him againe
(for hee was well aquainted with him when hee was in Scottland),
and for C. B. when ever hee came to towne hee would serve him
to the utmost of his power, for hee could nott butt beleeve hee was
deserving, since hee had my esteeme. Presently aftter this hee left
mee, and I expected hee would have laid aside all concerne for mee,
butt I soone found my mistake, and that I was in an error when I
beleeved hee loved mee att an ordinary rate, for itt was never more
visible then when hee had least hopes of a recompence, and changed
that afection to a vertuous freindship from wch att first hee might
have expected a lawfull injoyment.

Some time affter this I was advised to writte to C. B. to come to Ed[b]; w[ch] hee did as soone as was posible affter the receit of my letter, and had a lodging provided for him and his man in a private howse neere my Lord Tweedale's howse, where hee might come withoutt beeing scene upon the street. Every night in the close of the evening hee came in, and that was the time apointed where those persons mett with him who were contriving some meanes to asert there loyalty, and free there country from continuing inslaved. Those who most frequently mett was E. Dunfermeline, L[d] Belcarese, S[r] James H. and S[r] G. Mackery of Tarbott, who S[r] R. Moray had a great opinion of (though hee was then very young), and brought him into there caball as one whose interest and parts might make him very usefull to there designes. Affter they had formed itt in the most probable way to be succesfull, they found itt nesesary to bee armed with the King's authority for what they did, and therfore sentt to aquaint his Ma[tie] with what they intended, and to desire commission for severall persons nominate, and some blancke for such as might afterwards bee found fitt for the imploymentt. A few days affter these letters were sentt (the materiall part whereof was writt in white inck, and what was writt in ordinary incke was only to convey the other withoutt suspittion), S[r] G. Mack. came in to dinner to S[r] R. M. and told him hee had beene in a stationer's shop, and, taking up a booke accidentally, the first thing hee saw in itt was derection to writt withoutt beeing discovered, and there found the same way w[ch] they had beene making use of in there adrese to y[e] King, which putt them in some desorder; butt S[r] R. M. said the only hopes hee had was that if that booke came into the English hands, they would nott beleeve any thing so common as to bee in print would be made use of in any busynese of consequence; butt nott long affter they receaved an accountt of there letters comming safe to his Ma[ties] hands, and a full complying with there desire in sending the commissions with a safe hand to the North of Scottland, where those persons were to attend there arrivall. In the meane time S[r] G. M. was preparing

for his journy North, and C. B. was to goe with him under another
name, for hee needed noe other disguise, beeing knowne to none in
the kingdome butt those persons I have mentioned, who was too
much his friends and mine to have done him any prejudice. Amongst
all his aquaintance none proffest more freindship to him then S⁽ʳ⁾
James II. and made itt good in all circumstances wherein hee could
make itt apeare, giving him severall presentts usefull for the imploymentt hee was going aboutt, and a fine horse durable for service.
C. B. understood very well upon what accountt itt was that he receaved these testimonys of kindness, and did regrett the misfortune
of nott having itt in his power to obleige him, for hee knew noe
thing could doe itt more than his resigning his interest in mee, and
that was nott posible for him to doe, though hee would offten tell
mee if any thing should arive to deprive him of mee, hee thought
in gratitude I was obleiged to marry S⁽ʳ⁾ J. H.   I could nott butt
owne a very great sence of his civilitys, butt nothing could bee more
disagreeable to mee then speaking either in jest or earnest of my
marrying him, for nothing butt the death of C. B. could make mee
ever thinke of another (for what affter fell outt I had noe beleefe of,
and therfore could nott aprehend itt as a reason for my change).

The day beeing come apointed for S⁽ʳ⁾ G. M. and C. B. departure,
some interuption interveened, and therfore itt was delayed for a time.
Upon Christmas day [1652] an English woman who had beene a servantt to my Lady Belcarese (Sir R. M. lady's mother), according to
y⁽ᵉ⁾ English coustome, had prepared (in her owne house where shee
kept a change) better fare then ordinary, and amongst the rest a dish
of minced pies, of w⁽ᶜʰ⁾ when wee were att dinner shee brought over
two, and said one shee intended for S⁽ʳ⁾ Ro. and his lady, and the
other for S⁽ʳ⁾ J. H. (who was then there) and mee.   All the table
smiled att what shee said, butt I looked very gravely upon itt, and
rather wished itt with him that had more interest in mee.   All the
company beeing in a better humour then ordinary, wee were all
extreamely mery.   A woman beeing in the house called Jane Hambleton, who they say had the Second Sight, observing all very well

pleased, said to my Lady M's woman and mine, " There is a great
deale of mirth in this howse today, butt before this day eight days
there will bee as much sadnese;" wch too truly fell outt, for within 3
or 4 days my Lady Moray tooke her paines, butt they all struck
up to her hart, and all meanes beeing unsuccessfull shee died, with as
much regrett as any person could have.   Though her patience was
as great as was imaginable for any to have upon ye racke, and her
love to her husband great as her other qualiffications were, yett shee
earnestly desired death many howres before itt came; and S^r R.
satte constantly upon her bedside feeling her pulce, and exhorting
her cheerefully to indure those momentts of paine wch would soone
bee changed to everlasting pleasure.   And though noe doupt her
death was the greatest misfortune could arive to him, yett hee did
speake so excellently to her as did exceed by farre what the best
ministers said who frequently came to her; and was so composed
both att and affter her death, that neither action nor word could
discover in him the least of passion.   Hee imediately tooke care for
transporting her body to Belcarese, to bee bueried there with her
child, wch shee caried with her to her grave, beeing never seperated.
This was a sad lose to mee, for, besides the advantage I had in her
obleiging converse, I had the assistance of Sr R. advise in any
deficulty in my busynese, and hee wentt offtimes to consultations
with mee, and imployed his interest as farre as itt could bee usefull
to mee.   And when hee wentt away, hee very earnestly recomended
mee and my concernes to his cousin Sir J. Halkett, who was nott
ill pleased with the imploymentt.   This for some time putt a stop
to Sr G. M. going North, because Sr R. had some thoughts of going
with him; wch hee either did, or followed soone affter.

Upon Monday 7. of February, 1652-3, Sr G. M. and C. B. began
there journy from Ed.   The night before the E. of Dunfermeline
supt with him and mee att my chamber, and then ordered the way
of keeping corespondence, and what advise hee thought fitt for
the action hee was going aboutt.   Itt is nott to bee imagined butt
my trouble was great to part with him, considering the hazards hee

was exposing himselfe to, butt I must confese itt was increased by reflecting upon what Jane Hambleton had severall times said to Crew : that shee had observed a gentleman come privately to my chamber, and sayd shee knew that I and severalls looked upon him as one I intended to marry, butt hee should never bee my husband. And remembring how truly butt sadly fell outt what shee had foretold before, made mee the more aprehencive of this seperation, though I was one that never allowed my selfe to inquire or beleeve those that pretended to know future eventts.

I had of late beene so used to good company, that I was the more sencible now of the wantt of itt; and finding itt would bee more for my advantage to bee in some private howse, where my meatt might be dresed, then to have itt from the cookes, or keepe one for that use, therefore I resolved to take another lodging ; and having returned the furniture I borrowed, with my humble thanks for there use and the use of the howse, I tooke two roomes in Mr. Hew Walace howse in the foot of Blacke-fryar Wind.

Butt one remarkeable passage I mett with before I left the Earle of Tweedale's howse, wch I cannott butt mention. One evening, towards the close of daylight, there came a tall proper man into the roome where I was, and desired hee might speake to mee. I went towards him, and hee told mee hee was one who had nott beene used to seeke, butt now was reduced to that nesesity that hee was forced to aske my charity to keep him from starving. His lookes were so suitable to his words, that I could nott butt compasionate his condittion, and regrett my owne ; for all I had was butt one poore shilling, nor knew I where to borrow two pence. I thought to give him all I had might apeare vanity if any one should know itt, and to give him lese could nott suply his wantt, and therfore I resolved to give itt him all, and refferred my selfe to His hands for whom I did itt (concluding that perhaps some would lend mee y^t would nott give him); and I doupted nott butt God would provide for mee. So I gave him the shilling, which raised so great a joy in him that I could nott butt bee highly pleased to bee the instrumentt of that wch brought such praises to the God of Mercy; who left mee nott withoutt a recompence, for the next morning, before I was ready, the Earle of Roxborough came to my chamber, who was newly come from London, and brought mee a very kind letter from my sister, and twenty pound sterling for a testimony of her affection, wch I receaved as a reward for my last night's charity.

To make good the promise Sr J. H. made to Sr R. M. hee never came to towne butt I was the first person hee visitted, and was very solicitous in any of my concernes, and wentt with mee when I had occasion to attend ye Judges. I found frequency of converse increased what I was sory to find, and to devertt itt from my selfe I offten perswaded him to marry, and used severall argumentts from what hee had aquainted mee with in his owne condition, that made mee by way of freindship to him, and for preventing some inconveniences to his familly, very seriously advise him to marry; and I confese I proposed itt as a great sattisfaction to my selfe to have his condittion such as might make itt utterly imposible for him to have any thoughts of mee butt what might bee allowable to him in a maried state. I att last prevailed so farre with him, hee accknowledged hee was convinced itt would bee for his advantage to have a good discreet wife, and hee had had severall in his thoughts since I was so urgentt with him, and now was determined upon one, butt was resolved I should bee the first proposer of itt. I was very well pleased to undertake the imploymentt; and the way hee designed was by my recomending him by a letter to my Lord Belcarese, who had an interest in a handsome young widow, and to desire his Lord^p assistance to obtaine his designe. This hee did only to complementt mee; for his owne interest with my L. B. was much more then any I could pretend to, for hee had a great esteeme for Sr J.; and I remember once when I was att Belcarese (where I wentt frequently), my Lord was speaking something of Sr James, and I said, "Pray, my Lord, give mee leave to aske what the ground was that some people takes to speake with some reflection upon him?" "Truly (my Lord replied,) I beleeve

never person was more injured nor worse requited for a gallantt
action, and hee could nott have desired a better wittnese to vindicate
him then the King, for hee was a wittnese all the time standing
upon the leads of my Lord Belmerinoth's house att Leith, and saw
the whole proceedure; for, if itt had nott beene for Sʳ James and
those hee commanded, all the King's forces att that time att Musle-
brough had beene cutt off; and hee stood in the face of the enemy
while the rest retreated, and came handsomely off with very litle
disadvantage; and as I am a christian (said my Lord,) this is true;
and I have heard the King speake severall times of itt with great
aplause to Sʳ James, and anger att those who traduced him in what
was so eminently falce." And upon that occation hee heard the
King say, " Lord keepe mee from there malice! for I see they will
spare none they have a prejudice against."

To confirme that this humour did then very much reigne, I
cannott butt mention what I was a wittnese of my selfe. One day
Sʳ James came to see mee, and brought a gentleman with him who
hee beleeved much his freind; and affter severall discourses of
puplicke affaires, the gentleman satte sillent a litle while, and then,
smiling, said, " Sʳ James, now that I am convinced you are an
honest man, and love the King and his interest, I will make a con-
fesion to you. You were so great with my Lord Argile that I
thought itt imposible you could bee honest, and therfore I have
laine in my bed in a morning inventing some ill story of you, and
reported itt when I wentt abroad, and itt was joy to mee to have
itt beleeved; and, now I see my error, I aske your pardon;" wᶜʰ Sʳ
James soone gave, and past itt over as a jest.

Butt to returne where I left. Affter Sʳ James was resolved to
make adrese to that lady, hee intended to goe upon Monday the 21.
of March, 1652-3, to Belcarese, and desired to have my letter ready,
and in the morning hee would call for itt. I was nott long in
writting, and did recomend the designe to my Lord Belcarese with
as much earnestnese as the greatest concerne I could have, and had
the letter ready against hee came for itt, wᶜʰ was punctually yᵉ time

hee apointed. When hee came into my chamber, I saw something of joy in his face that I had nott observed in a long time; and I said I was glad to see him looke so well pleased, for had hee sooner resolved to goe a wooing, I had sooner scene a change in him. Though I saw him well pleased, yett I saw him in disorder with itt, and hee stood still a pritty while withoutt speaking a word. Att last hee said, " I have heard news this morning; and, though I know itt will trouble you, yett I thinke itt is fitt you should bee aquainted with itt. Just as I was turning downe Blacke-fryar Wind (said hee,) to come here, Coll. Hay called to mee, and told mee the post that came in yesterday morning had brought letters from London that undouptedly C. B. wife was living, and was now att London, where shee came cheiffely to undeceave those who beleeved her dead." " Oh! (said I, with a sad sigh,) is my misfortune so soone devulged?—

The leaf containing pages 101 *and* 102 *is lost.*

unworthy, and in what apeared so, none living could condemn mee more then I did myselfe. Butt I had some circumstances to plead for mee, withoutt wch I had beene unpardonable, and that was the concealing my intended mariage meerely because hee durst nott withoutt hazard of his life avowedly apeare, and therfore itt had beene imprudence to puplish what might have beene (in those times) ruine to us both.

As soone as I could get my selfe composed so as to goe abroad, I wentt where duty led mee more then inclination, for I aprehended every one that saw mee censured mee, and that was noe litle trouble to mee when I reflected on my misfortune that gave them butt too just grounds. Butt that I was with patience to suffer, and whatever els my Lord God thought fitt to inflict, to whom I did intirely submitt, and could make nothing unwellcome from His hand who had so wonderfully suported mee in so unparaleld a triall.

In May 1653 the Earle of Dunfermcline came to ·my chamber, and told mee hee had gott certaine information that there was a party of horse to bee sentt ye next day to Belcarese, and take my

Lord, and bring him prisoner to Ed^h, wch hee durst nott writt nor
communicate to any butt mee; and desired I would goe and lett
him know what was designed, that hee might escape; wch I undertooke, and wentt early the next morning, taking only a man with
mee (for I was nesesitate to leave my woman to looke affter some
busynese then fell outt); and the tide falling to bee betwixt 3 and 4
in the morning, and a very great wind, so as few butt the boatmen
and my selfe ventured to goe over, wch contributed well, for I landed
safe, and was att Belcarese before ten aclocke; and my Lord and Lady
wentt away imediately, and had desired mee to stay in the howse
with the chilldren, and take downe all the bookes, and convey them
away to severall places in trunkes to secure them (for my Lord had
a very fine library, butt they intrusted were nott so just as they
should have beene, for many of them I heard afterwards were lost).
I was very desirous to serve them faithfully in what I was intrusted,
and as soone as my Lord and Lady were gone I made locke up the
gates, and with ye helpe of Logan, who served my Lord, and one
of ye women, both beeing very trusty, I tooke downe all ye bookes,
and, putting them in trunkes and chests, sentt them all outt of the
howse in the night to the places apointed by my Lord, taking a
short way of inventory to know what sort of bookes were sentt to
every person; and with the toile and wantt of sleepe (for I wentt
nott to bed that night, and had butt litle sleepe the night before),
that I tooke the sodainest and the most violentt bloudy fluxe that
ever I beleeve any had in so short a time, wch brought mee so weake
in ten days time y^t none saw mee that expected life for mee. Butt
I forgott to tell that the things had nott beene two houres outt of
the howse when the troope of horse came and asked for my Lord.
There officer came up to mee, and I told him my Lord had beene long
sicke, (wch was true enough,) and finding itt inconvenientt to bee so
farre from the phisitians, was gone to Ed^b for his health. They
searched all the howse, and seeing nothing in itt butt bare walls and
weemen and chilldren, they wentt away. I gave accountt by an
exprese what I said according to there order, and affter some few

days staying conccaled att Ed^b, my Lord and Lady wentt to the North, and from thence wentt abroad.

I had sentt for my woman, who came the next day affter I fell sicke and prest much my sending for a phisitian; butt I knew none butt Dr Cuningham, and I could nott send for him because I knew hee was with my Ld Bel., and those phisitians who lived neere Belcarese was nott att home, so I concluded that the Lord had determined now to putt an end to all my troubles, and death was very welcome to mee. Only I beged some releefe from ye violentt paine I had, wch was in y^t extreamitty that I never felt any thing exceed itt. Butt itt seemes itt was only sentt for a triall, and to lett mee find the experience of the renued testimony of God's faver in raising mee from the gates of death. During my sicknese I was much obleiged to the frequentt visitts of most of ye ladys thereaboutts, butt particularly the Lady Ardrose; and Mr. D. Forett and Mr. H. Rimer seldome missed a day of beeing with mee. They were both pious good men, and there conversation was very agreeable to mee. As soone as I was able to goe outt and had beene att the church, the Lady Ardroses impertunity prevailed with mee to stay with her a weeke before I wentt to Edin^b; wch I did, and then, having taken my leave of all those whose civility to mee made itt nesesary, I returned to Ed^b; where I had nott beene long before Sr J. Halkett came to see mee, who had sentt often to inquire affter mee when I was at Belcarese, and excused nott comming himselfe, wch hee did refraine lest itt should occation discourse of that which hee knew would displease mee. I seemed nott to understand what hee mentt, neither was I curious to bee resolved; only thanked him for what hee had done and what hee left undone, for itt was nott reasonable for mee to expect a visitt from him att that distance. From the first day of my aquaintance with him I discovered a particular respect hee had for mee, and I have allready related what way I tooke to preventt ye increase of that wch could have noe hope of a suitable returne, and yett how obleiging hee was to that person who cheefely interrupted itt. Now that beeing, as hee thought, removed, I found by many

circumstances and inderect words that hee pleased himselfe with
what I never had a thought of; though I had beene highly ingrate
if I had nott had more than an ordinary value for him. Butt lest
hee should speake derectly to mee of what I knew too well and did
regrett, hee seldome was with mee that I did nott mention my
resolution never to marry, and that nothing kept mee from vowing
itt butt that I questioned if such vows were lawfull. The more hee
used argumentts to diswade mee from that resolution, I urged the
greatest reasons I had to confirme mee in itt; and att this rate wee
conversed severall months, hee seeking and I avoiding all occations
of his discovering his affection to mee. Att last, one day when hee
had beene some time with mee speaking of many variety of subjects,
when I least expected itt, hee told mee hee could noe longer conceale
the affection hee had for mee since the first visitt hee ever had made
mee, and had resolved never to mention itt had my condittion beene
the same itt was; butt now looking upon mee as free from all obligation to another, hee hoped hee might now pretend to the more
favor, having formerly preferred my sattisfaction above his owne.
I was much troubled att this discourse, wch hee could nott butt
observe; for ye teares came in my eyes. I told him I was sencible
that the civillity I had receaved from him were nott of an ordinary
way of friendship, and that there was nothing in my power that I
would nott doe to exprese my gratitude; butt if hee knew what disturbance any discourse like that gave mee hee would never mention
itt againe, "for as I never propose any thing of hapinese to my selfe
in this world, so I will never make another unhapy, and in this
denyall I intend to evidence my respect to you much more then if I
intertained your proposall, and therfore I intreatt you, if you love
either your selfe or mee, lett mee never heare more of itt." "Butt
(said hee,) I hope you will nott debarre my conversing with you."
"Noe, (replied I,) I will nott bee so much my owne enemy, and
upon the condittion you will forbeare ever to speake againe of what
you now mentioned noe person shall bee wellcomer to mee, nor any
will I bee willinger to serve when ever I have opertunity." Hee

said itt should bee against his will to doe anything to displease mee, butt hee would make noe promises.

A litle affter hee desired mee to lett his two daughters stay with mee, for hee designed to bring them to Ed^b to learne what was to bee taught there, and if I would lett them stay with mee hee would thinke himself obleiged to mee. I told him I had formerly promised him any service that lay in my power, and hee need nott doupt my performance; and if hee or they could dispence with what intertainementt I could give them hee needed nott doupt of there beeing wellcome, and itt would bee an advantage to mee to have so good company. His youngest daughter was butt a child, butt his eldest was neere a woman, and even then by more then ordinary discretion gave expectation of what since shee hath made good.

The lodging I was then in nott beeing convenientt for more then myselfe, I removed up to Mr. Glover's, att the head of Blackefriar Wind, where they and there woman came and staid with mee, and wee lived with very much quiett and contentt in our converse, Sr James cumming offten to see them, and bringing many times there unckle and cousin Sr R. Montgomery and Haslehead, who were both extreamely civill to mee and frequentt in their visitts.

Itt is so usuall where single persons are offten together to have people conclude a designe for mariage, that itt was noe wonder if many made the same upon Sr James and mee, and the more that his daughters were with mee. Butt I had noe thoughts of what others concluded as done, for I thought I was obleiged to doe all I could to sattisfy him, since I could nott doe what hee cheefely desired. I often desired him to dine and sup with his daughters, wch had beene a neglect if I had omitted, considering hee was often sending provision from his owne howse to them ; for hee knew I was nott of humour to take boord, nor did hee offer itt, butt made itt that way equivalentt, nott withoutt trouble to mee, for my inclination was ever more to give then receave.

Towards the winter hee staid most constantly att Ed^b, and then grew so importunate with mee, nott to allow his adrese, butt to give

him hopes that itt should bee succesfull, that to putt him past all
further pursuit I told him I looked upon itt as an addition of my
misfortune to have the affection of so worthy a person, and could
nott give him the returne hee deserved, for hee knew I had the tye
upon mee to another that I could nott dispose of myselfe to any
other if I expected a blesing, and I had too much respect to him to
comply with his desire in what might make him unhapy aud my
selfe by doing what would bee a perpetuall disquiett to mee. Hee
urged many things to convince mee that I was in an error, and
therfore that made itt void; butt when hee saw nothing could
prevaile, hee desired for his sattisfaction that I would propose itt
to Mr. David Dickson (who was one hee knew I had a great esteeme
of his judgementt), and rely upon his determination. This I was
contentt to doe, nott doupting butt hee would resolve the question
on my side.

The first time Mr. Dickson came to mee (wch hee usually did
once in a weeke), beeing alone, I told him I was going to comunicate something to him wch hitherto I had concealed, butt now
would entrust him with itt under promise of secresy, and beeing
impartially ingenious in giving mee his opinion in what I was to
aquaint him with; wch hee promising, I told him I did nott doupt
butt hee and his wife and many others in Ed^b did beleeve S^r Ja.
Halkett's frequentt visitts to mee was upon designe of mariage, and
I would avow to him that itt was what hee had offt with great
importunity proposed, and had a long time evidenced so reall an
affection for mee, that I could nott butt acknowledge if any man
alive could prevaile with mee itt would bee hee; butt I had beene
so farre ingaged to another that I could nott thinke itt lawfull for
mee to marry another; and so told him all the story of my beeing
unhapily deceaved, and what lengh I had gone, and rather more
then lese. Hee heard mee very attentively, and was much moved
att the relation, wch I could nott make withoutt teares. Hee replied,
hee could nott butt say itt was an unusuall tryall I had mett with,
and what hee praid the Lord to make usefull to mee. Butt with

all hee added that, since what I did was suposing C. B. a free person, hee nott proving so, though I had beene puplickely maried to
him and avowedly lived with him as his wife, yett, the ground of itt
failing, I was as free as if I had never seene him; and this, hee
assured mee, I might rely upon, that I might withoutt offence either
to the laws of God or man marry any other person when ever I
found itt convenientt; and that hee thought I might bee guilty of a
fault if I did nott when I had so good an offer. Hee used many
argumentts to confirme his opinion; wch though I reverenced comming from him, yett I was nott fully convinced butt that itt might
bee a sin in mee to marry, butt I was sure there was noe sin in mee
to live unmarried.

I was very just to Sr James in giving him an accountt what Mr.
Dickson had said, though nott till hee urged to know itt. And
beeing determined on what hee had offten pleaded, for hee hoped
now I would have nothing more to object, I told him, though hee
had made apeare lawfull to mee, yett I could nott thinke itt convenientt, nor could I consentt to his desire of marying withoutt
doing him so great prejudice as would make mee apeere the most
ungrate person to him in the world. I accknowledged his respect
had beene such to mee that were I owner of what I had just right
to, and had never had ye least blemish in my reputation (wch I could
nott butt suffer in considering my late misfortune), I thought hee
deserved mee with all the advantages was posible for mee to bring
him ; butt itt would bee an ill requitall of his civilitys nott only to
bring him nothing butt many inconveniences by my beeing greatly
in dept, wch could nott butt bee expected, having (except a hundred
pound) never receaved a peny of what my mother left mee, and had
beene long att law both in England and Scottland, wch was very
expencive, and I gave him a particular accountt what I was owing.
Yett all this did nott in the least discourage him, for hee would
have beene content att that time to have maried mee with all y^e
disadvantages I lay under ; for hee said hee looked upon mee as a
vertuous person, and in that proposed more hapinese to himselfe by

injoying mee then in all the riches of the world. Certainly none
can thinke butt I had reason to have more then an ordinary esteeme
of such a person, whose eyes were so perceptable as to see and love
injured vertue under so darke a cloud as incompassed mee aboutt.
When I found hee made use of all the argumentts I used to lessen
his affection as motives to raise itt higher, I told him since hee had
left caring for himselfe I was obleiged to have the more care of him,
wch I could evidence in nothing more then in hindring him from
ruining himselfe ; and therfore told him I would bee ingenious w^{th}
him, and tell him my resolution was never to marry any person till
I could first putt my affaires in such a posture as that if I brought
noe advantage where I maried, att least I would bring noe trouble,
and whenever I could doe that, if ever I did change my condittion,
I thought hee was the only person that deserved an interest in mee.
And this I was so fixt in that nothing could perswade mee to allter,
wch gave him both trouble and sattisfaction by delay and hopes.
Many proposalls hee made wherin hee designed to remove my
objections, butt though they were great expresions of his affection,
yett I would nott admitt of them ; butt they had this effect as to
make mee the sooner project the putting myselfe in a capacity to
comply with his desires, since I found they were unchangeable.
And I did resolve as soone as the winter session was done, wch I
expected would putt a close to my law-suite here, I would goe
to London, and vindicate my selfe from the suposed guilt I was
charged with, and then try what I could perswade my brother to
doe in order to the paying what I owed. I aquainted Sr James
with my intention, wch hee aproved of, since hee could nott perswade mee to nothing els.

Presently affter this Sr James came and shewed mee a letter hee
had receaved from London from the Countess of Morton, who very
earnestly desired him to come to her ; for shee had intrusted him
with the oversight of her jointure, and itt related to ye setling of
that and other things of concerne that made her impertunate for his
comming to her. Hee told mee my L. M. was a person who had

ever showne much respect to him, and that hee would willingly
serve her La.; butt the cheefe thing that would make him now
obay her commands was in hopes his beeing att London might bee
serviceable to mee if I would imploy him. I said, if his owne conveniency would allow of his journy, and that hee did incline to itt,
I would writte with him to my sister, who I would obleige to bee
civill to him upon my accountt, though hee deserved itt for his
owne. Within two days hee wentt, and I gave my sister such a
caracter of him as made his reception liker a brother then a
stranger. I refferred much to him to say wch was nott convenientt
to writte, and desired her to speake to my brother and give mee
accountt what I might expect of his kindnese in the proposall I
have lately mentioned, of which I expected noe answeare till
Sr James returned.

About a weeke affter hee was gone I fell into a feaverish distemper, wch continued some time, so y^t I found itt nesesary to send for
Doctor Cuningham, wch gave occasion to some people to say that I
fell sicke with heartbreake, because Sr James H. was gone to London to marry my Lady Morton; wch report wentt currantt amongst
some, though nott beleeved by any that was well aquainted with
any of the three; butt this aquainted mee with the humour of some
people, that use to make conclusions of there owne rather then
seeme ignorant of any thing. By the speedy returne Sr James
made hee convinced them of there folly who raised the reports, and
brought much sattisfaction to mee by the assurance I had from my
sister of beeing very wellcome to her whenever itt was convenientt
for mee to come, and till then shee thought itt best to delay speaking of any particular to my brother; butt for her husband I might
bee secure of his kindnese to bee ever the same I had found itt. Att
the same time I allso receaved severall letters from y^m who had
formerly had much friendship for mee, by wch I found itt had noe
abatementt by the late tryall I had mett with, wch did much
incourage-mee to kepe my resolution of going to London when ever
the season of the yeare would admitt of itt. In the meane time I

indeavered the settling of my busynese so as itt might receave noe prejudice by my absence; butt gott so many delays, yett dayly hopes of beeing putt to a close, that itt was the beginning of September '54 before I could take journy, wch I was much asisted to performe by the kindnese and favor of the old Countese of Dunfermeline, who invited mee to goe with her to Pinckey the Satturday before I was to goe for London, and beeing very inquisitive how I was provided for my journy, by my ingenuity her La^s found I was nott very certaine of what was convenientt, and upon the Monday when I was comming away my Lady brought mee ten pound, and said if shee had beene better provided shee would have lentt mee more, butt shee had borrowed itt of her Lord. I gave her La^s many thankes, who unasked had so civilly asisted mee, and desired to know whether I should make the note of my hand (wch I should send the next day) in my Lord's name or her La^s, and shee desired itt might bee in my Lord's name, wch accordingly I did, and paid since I was a widow.

The great civilitys I receaved from all Sr James H. relations made mee withoutt scruple goe to his sister to the Cavers the first night, where hee wentt with mee and his eldest daughter, who staid there till my returne. The youngest hee left att skole in Ed^b. Sr James wentt another day's journy with mee, and would have gone further, butt I would nott give him any further trouble, butt urged his returne, and wentt on my journy to Yorke, where I expected to meett the post coach, butt was disapointed, and forced to ride another day's journy. Sr James had an excellentt footman, who hee had promised my sister, and sentt him along with mee, who I gave mony to pay for his dictt and lodging affter we came to ye coach, because I thought itt not reasonable to expect hee could keepe up with itt. Affter wee had gone halfe the first day's journy, and the coachman driving att a great rate, I heard the coachman and postillian saying, " Itt cannott bee a man, itt is a devill, for hee letts us come within sight of him, and then runs faster then the sixe horses." So hee stops the coach, and inquires if any of us had a foot-

man. I told him I had. " Then (said he,) pray make much of him,
for I will bee answearable hee is the best in England." When I
found hee could hold outt (as hee did all the way), I made him run
by the coach; and hee was very usefull to all in itt. That journy
brought mee the aquaintance of S^r   Witherington and his
nephew Mr. Arington, who had one man; and my woman and my
selfe was all wee had in the coach. I had discharged my woman and
the footman to tell my name to any, butt tooke a borowed name.

S^r   beeing a very civill person, intertained mee with many
handsome variety of discourses, and related how hee had designed
to goe for Flaunders, and all his things a' ship-board, and while hee
was taking his leave the ship sett saile from Newcastle, and so hee
was forced to goe by land; wch fell outt well for mee, because I
could nott have mett with civiller gentlemen; butt I regretted to
find they were Roman Catholicks, and by my naming Mr. Fallowfield as one that I had scene, they presenttly knew who I was, and
said they would inquire noe further, for they had heerd him speake
of mee as one hee had soe great respect for, as that they would have
the same. This Mr. Fallowfield was an old priest that used some
time to come to N. Castle when I was there, and had offten writt
letters to mee for sicke persons, and highly complemented mee upon
there recovery. When I found they did know my name, I told them
the reason why I concealed itt was because I had beene long absentt
from my freinds, and there had beene many changes since I left
them, and therfore I resolved they should see mee before they heard
of mee.

Wee came to High Gate aboutt 2 a' clocke, where I desired to bee
left, and writt a note in with the footman to an old servantt of my
mother's to take a lodging in some private place in London, and to
come to mee the next morning with a coach; wch accordingly hee
did, and I wentt to White Fryars, where my brother Newton lodging used to bee, and most of those who desired nott to apeare puplickely. I then writt to my sister, who was then and her husband
att Warwick, by the footman Sr James II. had sentt her, aquaint-

ing her where I was, and that I intended to bee knowne to very few till I heard what shee advised mee to doe; for though I knew the Power that y^n governed did att that time indeavour to secure themselves rather by obleeging the Loyall party then ruining them, yett itt was cheefely to such who could doe them most prejudice, and so that was noe security to mee; besides ye dept I had was considerable, and therfore till I was sure they to whom itt was due would nott attempt any unhandsome action against mee, I thought itt was fitt upon both these considerations to conceale where I was, till I had some way secured myselfe from the inconvenience that I might suffer both upon a puplicke and private accountt.

My sister within three or four days returned backe the footman to mee againe with a very kind letter and twenty peeces, promising to bee with mee as soone as shee could, and till then thought itt best for mee nott to goe any where abroad. In the meane time I imployed my mother's old servantt to inquire of some that hee was aquainted with who ruled much in those times what there opinion was of my comming to London; butt there had beene so many changes among themselves, and some who they did much confide in who had left them beeing convinced of there error, that they looked now the more favorable upon those who had never beene on there side, and did more easily pardon what they acted against them. And this made mee the more secure as to the puplicke; and for my private troubles there was nott one who I was really owing any thing to butt they were as civill as I could desire, and as ready as ever to serve mee in what they had that could bee usefull to mee. Having thus farre sattisfied my selfe I only staid now till my sister came, that my going first abroad might bee with her, wch was shortly after. And having made some few visitts to some particular persons, I wentt with her and her husband to Charleton, wch was a howse of thers within 5 or 6 miles of London. My brother who lived then in the country with his familly came to see mee, and invited mee to his howse; where I wentt, and staid some time; butt my most constantt residence was with my sister, where I knew I was most wellcome to her and her husband; butt sometimes I wentt to London and had a lodging in Crew's mother's howse, where I staid when I had any persons to meett with, in order to setle what I came ther for.

One morning when I was there they brought mee word there was two gentlemen desired to speak with mee, who had brought a letter to mee from the Earle of Callander. I sentt for them up to my chamber, and did something wonder to find the man tremble when hee gave mee the letter, and his lips quiver that hee could hardly speake. I tooke the letter and read itt, concerning a busynese his Lorˢ had recomended to my care. I asked who brought itt from Scottland. Hee was nott well able to answeare mee, butt pointing to the other man, hee cam and arrested mee. I was strangely surprised, having never mett wᵗʰ nothing like itt, and asked att whose instance? Hee pointed to the other who had given mee the letter, and named him Mr. Maitland. I said I thought itt strange upon what accountt hee could doe itt, who I had never seene. Hee said itt was for a dept my brother Will owed his wife, and I promised to pay. I said itt was very strange I should promise to pay what I never till then knew was owing, nor did I ever heare of that woman's name till that time of my comming to London. Yett though all this was true I was forced to give baile, and to answeare att Guildhall, wᶜʰ I did by atturny Allen, and though they had hired a man of there owne to come and sweare that I had promised to pay the dept, yett hee so farre contredicted himselfe that itt was visible itt was a cheat, and the bill was flung over the barre ; wᶜʰ so exasperated yᵗ wicked woman that there was nothing imaginable that is ill shee did nott say of mee puplickely in the street, and the interest shee had with the soldiers, who was dayly drinking in her house att the Muse, made all people unwilling to medle with her. Butt I need nott insist upon this, wᶜʰ cost mee deare enough before I ended with her ; butt itt hath cost her dearer since, if shee did nott repentt, and if shee did, since the Lord hath forgiven her, I blese him for itt; so did I, as I sentt her word by her husband when I heard shee was dying.

I heard constantly once in a fortnight from Sʳ James, with many

renued testimonys that neither time nor distance had power to
change him.

I had nott beene long att London when I heard C. B. was come
there, who sentt to mee severall times to have leave to come once
butt to speake to mee, wch I as offten positively denyed as hee
earnestly asked itt. Butt one Sunday night, on the 10th of Decem-
ber '54, affter I had suped and was walking alone in my chamber,
hee came in, wch I confese strangely surprised mee, so that att
first I was nott able to speake a word to him. Butt a litle beeing
recollected, I said I thought hee had brought misfortune upon mee
enough allready, withoutt adding more to itt by giving new occation of my beeing censured for conversing with him. Hee intreated mee to give him leave butt to sit downe by mee a litle, and
hee would imediately leave mee; wch I did, and hee begun to
vindicate himselfe as hee had done offten ; butt I interupted him,
and told him though my charity would induce mee to beleeve him
inocentt, yett that could bee noe argumentt why I should now allow
him liberty to visitt mee, since hee could nott pretend ignorance of
that wch made mee thinke allowable once what were hainously
criminall now. Hee said hee desired mee only to resolve him one
question, wch was whether or nott I was maried to Sr J. H. I asked
why hee inquired. Hee said because if I was nott, hee would then
propose something that hee thought might bee both for his advantage and mine ; butt if I were, hee would wish mee joy, butt never
trouble mee more. I said nothing a litle while, for I hated lying,
and I saw there might bee some inconvenience to tell the truth,
and (Lord pardon the equivocation!) I sayd *I am* (outt aloud, and
secrettly said *nott*. Hee imediately rose up and said, " I wish you
and him much hapinese together ;" and, taking his leave, from that
time to this^a I never saw him nor heard from him; only when hee
had gott my writtings (of what concerned mee left to mee by my
mother) wch I had left with him when I wentt outt of London, and
hee had taken for security with him when hee wentt first to Holland

affter his escape outt of prison, that hee sent them to mee with a
letter.   The liberty hee tooke in comming outt from his concealed
lodging upon Sunday was upon an Act made by the Usurper, w^ch
was that none upon any accountt, what ever was there crime, should
bee aprehended upon that day, butt should have liberty to goe to
any church they pleased, or any other place; which shewed a veneration hee had for that day, though in other things hee forgott
obedience where itt was due by the same authority that comanded
that day to bee kept holy.   Butt when that hipocritte raigned y^e
people were insnared.

The first post affter C. B. had beene with mee, I gave S^r Ja. an
accountt of itt, who was so farre from beeing unsattisfied with itt,
that hee writt mee word if itt were nott that itt might doe mee
more prejudice in other people's thought then itt would doe in his,
hee would nott care though I dayly conversed wth him ; so litle did
hee aprehend any unhandsome action from mee, and therfore itt
had beene ye highest unworthynese and ingratitude to have beene
falce to so great a trust as hee reposed in mee.

I was above a twelvemonth indeavouring all I could so to setle
my affaires that I might have given Sr James some incouragementt
to come to mee, wch hee often designed to doe, butt I diswaded him
from itt till itt might bee with more sattisfaction to himselfe, for I
knew itt would bee butt a trouble to him to stay long att London
or returne withoutt mee, and the ill successe I had (in my proposalls
to my brother) would make one of them nesesary; butt Sr James
patience beeing long tried, hee would nott bee hindred any longer,
butt towards the latter end of the yeare 1655 hee came to London,
where I att that time had come for two or three days, and hee
returned with mee to Charleton to my sister's house, where hee
staid for the most part while hee continued in England.   The constancy of his affection, and the urgency of his desiring mee to marry,
made mee now unite all the interest I had either by relation or
freindship to gett mony, if nott to pay all I owed, yett such as was
most presing; and to accomodate my selfe in some way suitable for

what I designed, I imployed some againe to try my brother, who
(though one of the best natured men living) could nott bee prevailed
with either to lend or ingage for one peny for mee; butt I did nott
blame him, since the hindrance was from another hand, and that
disapointmentt came to make mee more highly value the kindnese
of my brother Newton, who voluntarily lentt mee three hundred
pound, and the Countese of Devonshire two hundred, wch was an
obligation that I shall never forgett, nor what paines Mr. Neale
tooke for mee to perswade her La^s, and was bound with mee to her
for the mony. I wish I had as much power to requite as I have
memory to retaine ye sence of those undeserved favors, and that my
reflecting upon them may raise up my thoughts to the adoration and
praise of Him who is the fountaine of mercy, and from whom
only all blesings are derived.

After this money was receaved and paid where itt was most nesesary, and y^t I had sattisfied all that I knew any thing was due to, I
wentt to London for some few days, where Sr James came to mee
in order to conclude our mariage, wch I could nott now in reason
longer deferre, since the greatest objections I had made against itt
was removed, and that I was fully convinced noe man living could
doe more to deserve a wife then hee had done to obleige mee; and
therfore I intended to give him my selfe, though I could secure him
of nothing more, and that was my regrett that I could nott bring
him a fortune as great as his affection to recompence his long expectation. Itt was nott withoutt many debates with my selfe that I
came att last to bee determined to marry, and the most prevalentt
argument that perswaded mee to incline to itt was the extreordinary
way that Sr James tooke even in silence to speake what hee thought
nesesary to conceale till itt apeared to bee fitt for avowing, and then
nott to bee discouraged from all ye inconveniences that threatned
his pursuit was what I could nott butt looke upon as ordered by the
wise and good providence of the Allmighty, whom to resist or nott
make use of so good an opertunity as by his mercy was offred to mee
I thought might bee offencive to his devine Matie, who in justice

might deliver mee up to the power of such sins as might bee a punishmentt for nott making use of the offer of grace to preventt them. And this consideration beeing added to Sʳ Jameses worth ended the contraversy. However, lest I might have beene mistaking, or Mr. D. Dickson in his opinion, who thought itt lawfull for mee to marry, I entred nott into that state withoutt most solemne seeking the determined will of God, wᶜʰ by fasting and prayer I suplicated to be evidenced to mee, either by hedging up my way with thornes that I might nott offend him, or that hee would make my way plaine before his face, and my paths righteous in his sight. And as I beged this with the fervor of my soule, so itt was with an intire resignation and resolution to bee contentt with what ever way the Lord should dispose of mee. To this I may add Sᵗ Paul's attestation, " The God and Father of our Lord Jesus Christ, wᶜʰ is blesed for evermore, knoweth that I lie nott." (2 Cor. xi. 31.)

Affter this day's devotion was over, every thing that I could desire in order to my mariage did so pleasingly concurre to the consumation of itt, and my owne mind was so undisturbed and so freed of all kind of doupts, that with thankefullnese I receaved itt as a testimony of the Lord's aprobation, and a presage of my future hapinese; and, blesed bee his name! I was nott disapointed of my hope. Upon Satturday the first of March, 1655-6, Sʳ James and I wentt to Charleton, and tooke with us Mr. Gaile, who was chaplaine to the Countese of Devonshire, who preached (as hee some times used to doe) att the church the next day, and affter super hee maried us in my brother Newton's closett, none knowing of itt in the familly or beeing presentt butt my brother and sister and Mr. Neale ; though, conforme to the order of those that were then in power, who allowed of noe mariage lawfull butt such as were maried by one of there Justices of Peace, that they might object nothing against our mariage, affter the evening sermon my sister pretending to goe see Justice Elkonhead who was nott well, living att Woolwitch, tooke Sʳ James and mee with her in the coach, and my brother and Mr. Neale wentt another way affoott and mett us there,

and the Justice performed what was usuall for him att that time,
wch was only holding ye Derectory in his hand, asked Sr James if
hee intended to marry mee, hee answered Yes ; and asked if I
intended to marry him, I said Yes. Then says hee, " I pronounce
you man and wife." So calling for a glase of sacke, hee drunk and
wished much hapinese to us; and wee left him, having given his
clarke mony, who gave in parchmentt the day and wittneses, and
attested by the Justice that hee had maried us. Butt if itt had nott
beene done more solemnly afterwards by a minister I should nott
beleeved it lawfully done. Affter I was maried I staid butt a short
while with my sister, and concealed my mariage from all except
some particular persons that either relation or freindship made mee
have confidence of, for itt was nott a time for any that honored the
King to have any puplicke celebration ; and another reason for per-
forming itt privately was that aboutt ten days before I was maried
Mrs. Cole, who was Maitland's wife, had arested mee againe, and I
was forced to give in new baile, who were such as I owned my intention of marying, and going imediately affter for Scottland, and
obliging my selfe to keepe them harmelese. I left the managementt
of itt to him who before I had imployed for my atturny, who was
so confidentt shee could never recover two pence of mee that hee
said hee would bee contentt to pay what ever should bee determined
by the judges against mee, for hee said hee could prove by very
good wittneses that shee said (when her former bill was cast over
the barre), " Well, I will have one that shall sweare to the purpose,
though I should give him ten pound for his paines." Hee beeing
an understanding active man, and giving mee such assurance, made
mee with the lese disturbance leave London, for if I had had any
aprehension of what affter fell outt I might have easily prevented
ye prejudice shee did mee; for 3 yeare affter my atturny died,
and my baile beeing in ye country, shee gott outt a judgementt
against mee privately, so that none ever heard of itt that was
concerned in mee. And though itt cost mee a great deale of
trouble and expence (wch to this day I am owing for to Mr. Neale)

to had (*sic*) that judgement reduced, yett found itt imposible, because itt was confirmed by the Act of Indempnity, made by the King when his M^tie first came home, wch was much outt of my way, as well as injurious to many others. Butt that was my misfortune, wch I had felt the weight of more heavily if att the same time the King had nott beene graciously pleased to grant mee 500 pound outt of ye Exchequer. Butt of this I shall have more occasion to speake hereaffter.

Sr James and I having taken leave of our friends, came safe withoutt any ill accidentt (in the post coach) the lengh of Bow Bridge, within   mile of Yorke ; and there wee had so remarkable a deliverance that I cannott omitt the relation of itt. There was none in the coach butt Sr James and I, his man and my woman, and a big fatt gentleman whose name I forgott, butt hee was one that had imploymentt under the Bishop of Durham. Aboutt a quarter of a mile before wee came to the bridge that gentleman had lighted outt to walke a litle, and came in and satt on the side of the coach wch was contrary to the place hee was in before, wch contributed much to our safety, for Sr James and hee beeing on the one side of ye coach, and his man in that boot, Crew's weight and mine was the less considerable, who were next to ye danger. Butt all of us had unevitable beene drowned and had our neckes broke, withoutt an extreordinary providence; for 6 horses beeing in ye coach, and the postillion nott carefull how hee entred the bridge, wch was butt narrow, withoutt any ledges upon itt, and built of the fashion of a bow, from wch itt had the name, hee driving carelesly, both the wheeles of that side where I satt wentt over ye bridge, which the coachman seeing, cried out, " Wee are all lost," and flung himselfe outt of the coach boxe, and to escape hurt his leg very ill, so that hee could hardly gett up to pull the horses to him ; nor was there scarce roome upon the bridge to give any assistance. Butt that wch was our preservation was some good angell I thinke (sentt by his Master), who, seeing the danger wee were in, held the coach behind all the way till itt was off the bridge. Itt was so extreordinary a deliverance that wee knew nott how to bee thankefull enough to God Allmighty who had given itt, butt resolved to reward the man who had beene instrumentall in itt; butt when wee all came outt of the coach att the end of the bridge, and inquired for ye man, there was none to be seene, nor had wee all that day mett or overtaken any travailer, only that man was seene by Ilary Macky and the coachman to hold up the coach along the bridge, butt they both declared they never saw him before nor affter ye danger, and that wch made itt apeare the more strange was that hee seemed to bee butt a poore man, and such doth nott usually doe any service withoutt seeking a recompense. Butt whatever hee was, itt was hee the Lord made use of as a meanes of our safety, and the less wee knew of his comming, the more wee had reason to bee thankefull to Him who brought him there. When wee came to Yorke, and related what wee had escaped, itt was the admiration of all that heard itt. The coachman and postillion was very penitentt for there fault, and therfore wee forgave them; butt would make noe more use of them, for wee hired another coach to Newcastle, where Sr James had apointed his owne horses and servantts to meett him, because hee intended to see his sisters as hee wentt home, wch hee did, and wee came safe withoutt any other accidentt to the Cavers, where I was receaved with much kindness by all, butt most from Sr Jameses daughter, who I had left there, and was very well pleased to returne home with mee, wch shee did affter some days stay att Cavers.

When wee came to Edb, I sentt my excuse for nott beeing fitt then to waite upon my Lady Broghill, who was then there with her Lord, who was Presidentt of the Counsell, butt resolved to come there againe only to pay that respect wch I had for them both, nott as they were then imployed, butt as I had long beene intimately aquainted with them before, and knew that what they acted now was more outt of a goode designe than an ill, as was evidentt by the civility they shewed to all ye Royallists. Affter wee came home, and

had receaved a very kind wellcome from all Sr James his friends
and neibours, and that wee were a litle setled, hee thought itt convenientt for us to goe over, as I promised, to waite upon my Lady
Broghill; and the reason wch made Sr James the sooner doe itt was,
that severall gentlemen who had ingaged to serve under the English
power in puplicke imploymentt as Justices of Peace had presed to
have Sr James one of that number, butt hee declining, they made
his name bee inserted in the list, with this certification, that whoever
refused to act in that station who was nominate should bee sentt to
ye Castle att Ed^b. This made us hasten our journy; and as soone
as wee came there, a gentleman (who I will nott now name, because
I hope hee repents what hee then did,) that had beene very urgentt
with Sr James to accept ye imploymentt, came and importunately
presed him againe, and, to make mee ye better sattisfied with the
proposall, told mee many advantages hee would receave by itt, and
was very desirous that hee might goe with mee to make my aquaintance with my Lady Broghill. I excused my going att such times
as hee mentioned, only because I would nott have him with mee,
nor did I take notice as if I had ever seene her. Butt as soone as I
was free of him I wentt presenttly affter dinner.

They lay then in the Earle of Muray howse in the Canon Gate,
and just as I came in att ye gate my Lord Broghill was going outt,
and with him a great attendance, and amongst the rest y^t gentleman
who had beene so forward to have Sr James putt in to bee a Justice
of Peace. Hee was a litle surprisd when he saw my Lord Br. come
with so much freedome and kindnese and bid mee wellcome, and
bringing mee to ye staires, asked if I had any service for him. I
said, " My Lord, though there hath beene many sad changes since I
saw your Lor^p, yett I still look upon you as the same person you
were, and therfore in short I am come to beg your Lo^p faver to S^r
James, who I heare is in the list." " Why! (said hee,) hath hee
nott a mind to be a Justice ?" " Noe, my Lord, so farre from itt,
that hee will goe to ye Castle first." " Well, my word for it, (replied

hee,) you shall never heere of itt more." Beeing then in hast, going up to some committee, hee left mee with his Lady, and ingaged me to dine with them ye next day; wch I did, and had all ye assurance I could desire that Sr James should bee free from having any thing imposed upon him that was contrary to the duty and Loyalty that became a faithfull subject.

Affter two or three days stay in Ed^b wee returned home, and presently affter came the order to Sr James either to joyne with the other Justices of Peace or goe to the Castle. When I saw itt I confese I was much disordred, and the more because I had such confidence of my Ld B. word. I desired Sr James to tell the mesenger that ye next weeke hee would doe one of them if desired, and imediately I writt a letter to my Lord B. telling how much I was surprised with that order, affter I had his Lor^p promise to have

(*Cætera desunt.*)

APPENDIX.

MEDITATIONS.

Upon the Fast which by Proclamation was kept Jan. 30, 1660-1.

This is a day on which the greatest murder was committed that ever story mentioned, except the Crucifying of our Saviour.

＊　　　＊　　　＊　　　＊　　　＊　　　＊

Had nott his Majesty [a] come under all those tryalls and sufferings, how should the world and his owne subjects have knowne his piety, patience, his meekenese and his charity, his constancy in suffering, and the heavenly ejaculations which upon all occations hee offred up to God in his solitudes ? Which like monuments are left to future generations to teach them how to follow what was eminent in him.

＊　　　＊　　　＊　　　＊　　　＊　　　＊

The Scotts are blamed, and surely they deserve itt, if itt were butt for being too credulous; butt lett them that are withoutt this sin of being guilty of the King's murder in the Three Nations cast the first stone att the other, for either simply, willfully, or passively all are guilty, and therfore all had need to bee humbled greatly for so hainous a transgression.

＊　　　＊　　　＊　　　＊　　　＊　　　＊

Upon the death of my deare Son Henry, being the 12 *of May,* 1661.

What a sad journy hath this beene hether to mee into England where I expected greatest sattisfaction : 1st. in seeing the King and Royall family restored, and then in seeing my relations and friends ; and to mitigate these joys the Lord is pleased dayly to send mee new afflictions,

[a] Charles the First.

and to take away allmost the cheefe comforts of my life, which is my
deare children, the first as being best beloved, and this as next succeed-
ing, and all to teach mee nott to love the world or anything that is in
itt. I was nott a wittnesse of my deare Hary's suffering as I was of his
sister's, butt by relation itt was a long lingring sicknese, every day
threatning death, and att last it came, to putt an end to his mortality
just in the night of that day of the weeke (beeing Sunday ᵃ) that hee first
receaved breath; and had hee lived one month longer hee had beene
just three yeare seeing the world and feeling the bitternese of itt, for
seldome had hee health to make him sencible of those joys which accom-
pany every age, for every one hath something suitable to itt where the
blesing of health is to make them sencible of them.

*   *   *   *   *   *

Upon making vows.

I never was in any affliction or distresse butt I was apt to make vows,
and I noe sooner was delivered butt I forgott them. Even lately I have
had experience of my selfe; for, having long since vowed that if I could
live to see that day on which the crowne should be sett upon the King's
head, I would, during my life, make that a day of particular devotion for
blesings upon him, and yett for all there hath beene butt fou Tuesdays
past by mee, yet halfe of them I have nott remembred till they were past,
which makes mee now resolve never to vow anything againe butt to bee
humbled, that I cannott performe them as I would, and as the benefitts
require.

Upon the disbanding of the Army, and the disorder that followed.

Who is now living that did ever expect to see this day? That so
great and so successful an army, who gave laws to Three Kingdomes and
cutt off there lawfull King, that set up and pulled downe who they pleased,
that this army should be disbanded withoutt any resistance only by the
vote of King and Parliament.

ᵃ Sunday, the 13th of June, 1658, as in p. 57 of the same volume.

Sure itt would apeare these people's inclinations were to bee obedient if they had had such officers and rulers as would have shewed them good example, butt mostt generally the multitude is like an impetuous innundation, which runs most violently any way itt takes. Therfore they are wise who can sett them forward towards what is good and allowable, and then unquestionably they will run like a well biased bowle that way itt is derected by the thrower. Men may imagine reasons to themselves for these late unheard of changes, from good to ill, and from ill to good againe; butt certainly the hand of God is visible in all these alterations. Els how could itt have beene posible for a good and a greatly beloved King to have beene murdered publickly before his owne gates by a handfull of people (in comparison of the rest), and none made resistance butt with sighes and teares? How could this have beene done had nott the Lord for a just punishment of our sins taken from us power, strength, and wisdome?

How could the vilest of the people beene submitted to by so many better then themselves, who complied with them, had nott God taken from them there reason and there honor?

How could so many men have lost there lives both in England and Scotland for intending to restore the King and owning of his interest, and then to have him brought home in peace by the unanimous desire of the generallity of the people? how could this have beene done butt by that God who only doth determine of life and death and times and seasons?

There is a time for all things, says the wise man (Eccles. iii. 1); there was a time for the King to suffer exile, and all his subjects to bee enslaved, and a time for him to bee restored; butt till this time came that God had apointed for itt all industry was fruitlese.

Now itt seemes this was the time and by this meanes that this army was to bee disbanded, and from this many expected peace and quiett, which they thought could nott bee as long as such men were in armes that had done so much against the royall power.

"Scatter the people that delight in warre," was a prayer made long since by the Psalmist (Psalm lxviii. 30); and now wee see that prayer made good so many ages after to lett us see there never was a prayer putt up in faith, either from a person or people, butt had a returne att some time or other. Butt to lett us see the rules we prescribe our selves, as meanes to attaine our ends, proves most times the contrary (yett ought none from this forbeare to doe what's most agreeable to reason, and leave the success to Him who makes all things worke together for good to them that feare Him). The disbanding of this army was looked upon as a thing impossible without great mutiny; and the keeping it together seemed very dangerous; and yett how willingly every man went to his owne home att these severall days of dicipation, with the apearance of joy and acclamation, and praying for the King, who liberally rewarded there last actions though there former had beene so rebellious.

From this, which some made a ground to expect peace, others take occation to raise disturbance, and are nott afraid to intitle God to bee the owner of there quarrell and rebellion; but Hee who sitts in Heaven will laugh at there folly, and make them a derision unto all that hate them, because they have blaspheamed the name of the Most High and rebelled against the Lord and His anoynted.

1660-1, *January* 6, 7, 9. What disturbance hath those men made these three nights in one of the most populous and best governed cittys in the world! and yett they are butt a handfull in comparison of the multitude that were against them; butt a gangreue in the least degree begun hazords the lose of the whole body if not cutt off in time, and, since the multiplied mercys of a gracious and indulgent King cannot reclaime them, his severity must be made use of, and by letting bloud to purge outt that coruption which els might be infectious.

     *   *   *   *   *   *

Upon the meeting that was to determine of Church goverment, being upon Tuesday, 3ᵈ of November, 1661.

This day the Parliament hath apointed to debate or determine of the goverment of the Church, or more properly, I may say, to determine of those ministers who will nott bee conforme to the goverment allready intended to bee established, for I cannot say it is firmely established when in most parts of the kingdome itt meets with oposition. Questionlese the generallity of the kingdome is inclined to Episcopisy as being the ancient goverment of this Church, and what many of the laws are built upon; yett that will nott persuade others to bee of there judgement, because they are posesed with a prejudice against it. There may bee ill Bishops, butt that should be looked upon as they are men, and nott bring a disrespect upon there function, for what man living is withoutt sin?

*   *   *   *   *   *

In fundimentalls both agree, Episcopall and Presbiterian, and yett none more violent then they one against another for the shadow; for such is the name of Bishop or ceremonys in comparison of that truth which is the substance. Did both sides seeke sincearly the glory of God, and the salvation of the soules committed to there charge, they would imploy themselves better then to make disturbances to the distruction of many soules as well as bodys. Were there a holy emulation which should come neerest to there head and master the Lord Christ, who said, "Learne of mee, for I am meeke and lowly in hart," (Matthew xi. 29,) then undoubtedly they should obtaine what follows,—they should have rest unto there soules, and should nott only have peace, butt many blessings that attend itt.

*   *   *   *   *   *

To conclude these meditations concerning the King, I am fully perswaded the Lord hath designed him to bee an heire of glory and an instrument of much praise to himselfe by being a reformer both by his lawes and his practise, and till the time come I will dayly pray for the hastening of itt: and as his Majesty shewed great magnanimity and courage in his undaunted resolution of being crowned the apointed day, though the phanatickes, both in words and papers flung into the King's court att Whitehall, had with much boldness affirmed as from some inspiration that the crowne should never be sett upon his head, and that from these threats and more deliberate thoughts some faithfull to his Majesties interests did endeavour to diswade from keeping the intended day for coronation, because itt fell to bee a day on which there was an eclipse of the sun, and that might confirme some in there thoughts of his Majesties unhappy reigne; butt to this the King would nott condescend, butt with a Christian fortitude replied hee feared neither the threats nor the omen, because hee knew the Lord overuled all such events, and therefore hee would keep his first resolution and rely upon God for his blesing and preservation.

And that the God of power and glory may be praised I must record what I was witness of my selfe when his Majestie ridd from the Tower to Whitehall the day before the coronation, which was one of the greatest solemnitys that I believe ever Brittaine saw. Though the King had great and royall attendance and faithfull sarvantts, yett such was the multitude of beholders that crouded in aboutt the King that his sarvants were nott able to keepe aboutt the horse on which his Majestie did ride, and I saw very many meane ordinary persons laying there hands upon the horse and the rich trapings, which putt mee into that terrour for feare of some attempt upon his Majesties person that itt tooke away the satisfaction that els I should have had in so glorious a sight; butt I turned my feares into prayers, and was heard in that I feared, and the Lord granted my requests, and none had power to hurt him, praised be the Lord of mercy for it! Butt while I was thus conflecting with my feares the King rode on with a serene undisturbed composure, free either from feare or vanity, and seemed to be pleased with the liberty the rude multitude tooke to aproach him, who certainly was restrained trom there ill designes by the same spiritt that said, *Toutch nott my Anointed.*

The next day, being Tuesday, his Majestie was crowned, nottwithstanding all the oposition threatned by the phanatikes; and some time affter coronation there was the most terrible tempest of thunder, lightening, and raine that ever I saw, so that I feared some danger to his Majestie in his returne from Westminster coming by watter to Whitehall, where I waited, and had the honor to have the first kiss of his Majesties hand affter coming into the Howse; and on my knees, with an uplifted hart and soule, I· beged that God would crowne his Majestie with all the blessings both of heaven and earth, for I was transported to see the King come sodainely into the room where I was alone waiting and praying for his Majesties safe arrivall, for the storme was such as if his enemys had conspired with the Prince of the power of the aire; butt for that day's mercy to the King I did resolve (and have hitherto kept itt) upon every Tuesday to make a solemne accknowledgement of the mercy in giving God thankes for setting the crowne that day upon his Majesties head, and in most humble fervent intercessions and suplications for his Majesties long, holy, and prosperous raigne.

One remarke I must nott omitt, which was, after the crowne had beene sometime upon the King's head, the weight of itt made his Majesties head to acke, for which he tooke itt off and held itt in his hand; and some from that made presages of the short continance of his Majesties raigne; butt, oh! how unreasonable and irreligious is all such observations! Had I beene wittness of that (which my being great with child made mee nott venture into such a crowd) I had interpreted rather that his Majestie tooke off his crowne with reverence to adore the King of Kings, who had sett itt on his head, in imitation of the fowre and twenty Elders who cast there crownes before the throne, saying, " Thou art worthy, O Lord, to receave glory and honor and power, for Thou hast created all things, and for thy pleasure they are and were created;" and noe doubt butt as the weight of itt upon his Royall head putt him in mind of the great and weighing cares that attend a crowne, so the taking itt off was with an offering itt up and himselfe to the Lord and seeking a blessing upon his people and himselfe, and that that crowne might bee a pledge to him of that etternall crowne that fadeth nott butt continueth for ever. These and such like I believe were his Majesties thoughts during that solemnity.

*　　　*　　　*　　　*　　　*　　　*

Meditations and Resolutions upon Luke ii. 36, 37, *and* 38 *verses.*

(P. 51.) For though I did not talke away sermons as too too many did (which the Lord pardon), yett that is an agravation of my guilt, that I saw that sin in them, and did nott amend it in myselfe the secrett wandrings of my heart, which tooke mee vp as much from hearing as there discourses did them.

(P. 64.) When I was young, I fasted weekely every Wednesday from the example of a lady, whom I believe did itt outt of a pious consideration, butt I had then noe other reason butt only to shew I could forbeare all kind of sustenance twenty-four hours ; butt as I grew older and more acquainted with my duty I found fasting a great helpe to prayer and humiliation, and in the yeare 1644 I did then wholy sett apart that day for seeking mercy to reconcile the sad differences that was betwixt the King and his people and to mourne for the sins that occationed itt. Sometime when seriously I wentt aboutt that dutty I have felt the peace which paseth all natturall understanding, and so for a long time I continued itt; butt when I att any time made a mocke of itt by only forbearing to eate, butt nott forbearing to sin, then was itt truly made a day for mee to mourne for while I have life.

Since I grew old I found fasting prejudiciall to my health, and therfore I laid itt aside, as believing our Lord would pardon the omitting what I was nott well able to performe, and since though I do nott fast every Wednesday, yett I make that still a day of confession of the sins I was guilty of when I did fast, and since I did forbeare. And every Satturday now, since that day the Lord made mee a widow, I have endeavord to spend itt in holy abstenance and retirement. And how to improve itt more shall bee now my care and to try all ways how to serve the Lord with fasting and prayers night and day.

Kneeling in Prayer.

Though in this Church that cousttem is outt of use of kneeling in the time of prayer, and that for the most part all the congregation sitts rather like judges or auditors then those that were making suplication, as if they had so farre committed there cause to the minister's prayer that they need neither joyne with him themselves nor add anything for there owne nesesitous condittion, Lord convince them of the evil of this way that are guilty off itt.

INDEX.